POLITICAL POISON

POLITICAL POISON • BY MARK RICHARD

A

P a u l

T u r n e r

M y s t e r y

ZUBRO • ST. MARTIN'S PRESS NEW YORK

Mark Richard Zubro

POLITICAL POISON. Copyright © 1993 by Mark Richard Zubro. All rights reserved. Printed in the United States of America. No part of this book may be used or reproduced in any manner whatsoever without written permission except in the case of brief quotations embodied in critical articles or reviews. For information, address St. Martin's Press, 175 Fifth Avenue, New York, NY 10010.

DESIGN BY JUDITH A. STAGNITTO

Library of Congress Cataloging-in-Publication Data

Zubro, Mark Richard.
    Political poison / Mark Richard Zubro.
        p.   cm.
    ISBN 0-312-09364-0 (hardcover)
    ISBN 0-312-11044-8
    I. Title.
PS3576.U225P65   1993
813'.54—dc20   93-17035
                                                                                    CIP

First Paperback Edition: May 1994

10 9 8 7 6 5 4 3 2 1

To the traveling road crew: Barb, Debbie, and Mike.

A C K N O W L E D G M E N T S

For their kind assistance: William B. Kelley, Gerald Hannion, Jr., Paul Varnell, James White, Mike Rockwell and Commander Hugh Holton, Chicago Police Department

And to that old gang of mine—thanks once again to: Kathy Pakieser-Reed, Michael Kushner, Rick Paul

O N E

I'm going to slide on over to our witness on Fullerton and then head home," Buck Fenwick announced.

In the Chicago Police Department the detectives never "drove" anywhere. Usually they "slide," sometimes they "drift" over. The last Chicago cop who drove anywhere was a rookie three years ago, and he simply didn't know any better.

Paul Turner nodded at his partner and glanced at the clock over the rumbling radiator. For the first time in two weeks he'd be going home from Area Ten headquarters at four-thirty, exactly on time.

Minutes later Paul drove home straight down Halsted, through Greektown, skirted the University of Illinois campus, then west on Taylor Street. Two blocks later he turned right and into his garage.

In the kitchen he gulped down a large glass of orange juice.

He heard the thump of feet down the stairs and moments later his son Brian appeared in the kitchen doorway. His seventeen-year-old wore white socks, faded jeans, and a white t-shirt that bulged over his chest and shoulder muscles. Soon the boy would catch up with his dad.

Brian whispered, "You better talk to Jeff."

"Why are you whispering?" Paul asked.

"I'm serious, Dad. Something's bothering him, and he won't tell me what."

Jeff, Turner's eleven-year-old, worshipped his older brother. Their rare fights were quickly over and forgotten.

"When did it start?" Paul asked.

"I thought it was because he tripped on his way into the house. He swung his crutch at me when I tried to help him up."

Jeff had spina bifida, a birth defect that the three of them had come to terms with, though it had taken many years of struggle. These days Jeff was to the point of handling the occasional falls and frustrations of maneuvering on crutches and in wheelchairs with a grimace and a shrug.

"He hit you?" Paul asked.

"It's not a big deal, Dad, but I'm worried about him. He wouldn't talk to me. He tells me stuff he doesn't tell you, but I can't get a word out of him."

Paul found Jeff in the den in front of the Nintendo set. Jeff frequently beat both his older brother and his father at a wide variety of electronic games. The screen showed the beginning of the Tengen edition of the Tetris game, which Jeff preferred to the Nintendo version. The screen finished the opening explanation of how to play, but Jeff didn't click the controls to begin. Late April afternoon sunlight streamed through gauze curtains, continuing to fade the spot under the window.

Paul knelt next to the worn, golden overstuffed chair and touched his son's arm. Jeff flinched, and he wouldn't make eye contact.

2

"What's wrong, Jeff?" he asked.

No answer.

Paul asked, "Did something happen at school? Should I call your teacher?"

"No," Jeff murmured.

"Are you physically hurt? Should I call the doctor?"

Jeff shook his head.

Paul waited a few moments, trying to figure out what he could say to get his son to talk. He said, "You aren't playing your game. I've got time for a couple tries."

Jeff shrugged.

"You hit your brother. You can't do that, Jeff. You know it's wrong."

Jeff glanced at his father. Paul saw a tear in the boy's eye. "I didn't mean to hit him," he whispered. "Is he mad at me?"

Paul put his arm around his son. The boy didn't flinch, but Paul could feel tension in the slender shoulders. He said, "No, he loves you. He's concerned about you. So am I. What's wrong?"

Jeff gulped and drew a deep breath. He reached a hand for his dad's arm. Paul caressed his son gently. Jeff said, "Dad, are you going to die?"

The question startled Paul. Carefully considering possible responses, he finally asked, "Why do you ask?"

Jeff hesitated and then all the words came out in a rush. "At school today one of the kids said all gay people are going to die of AIDS and on television all the gay people have AIDS and they all die. You aren't going to die, are you, Dad?"

Paul had told both his sons about his sexual orientation when they were ten years old. He wanted to be honest, and to tell them before they heard it from someone else. He and Brian were closer than most fathers and sons, and Paul always put down a large part of this to his honesty about his sexuality. He'd told Jeff last year, and he thought the boy was handling it well. Today's question was something new.

Paul knelt in front of his son. Tears flooded the boy's eyes. Paul brushed the hair back on his son's forehead, placed his hands on the boy's arms.

"Television shows are just pretend, aren't they?" Paul asked.

The boy sniffed and nodded.

"And we've talked about how your friends don't always have accurate information?"

Jeff nodded. He'd been through a lot with kids and even adults with misinformation and ridicule about his birth defect.

"We've talked about AIDS, haven't we?"

Another sniff and nod.

"You know I was tested and the results were negative. That means I don't have the antibodies and that I'm okay."

"Then why do they only put gay people who are sick on television?" the eleven year old asked.

"Television doesn't put very many gay people on its programs."

"Why not?" his son demanded.

"I don't know, Jeff. They just don't, but there's lots of gay people. Uncle Ian, Ben Vargas. You know them. They aren't dying and neither am I."

Paul looked into his son's brown eyes, the thick dark eyelashes which showed his Italian heritage. "Feel better?" he asked.

The boy visibly relaxed. He put his arms around his dad, and they hugged. They played three games of Tetris. Paul insisted they quit when Jeff reached level ten.

Over dinner Paul told them about an incident earlier in the day at a jewelry shop on Wabash Avenue in the Loop. He'd been part of a foot chase that ended up at Buckingham Fountain.

"Did you get shot at?" Jeff asked.

"One of the crooks some other detectives were chasing fired one shot in their direction. Nobody got hurt." He could have lied or told them nothing, but the incident would very likely be on the evening news. He'd rather they hear it from him.

"Did you have your vest on?" Jeff asked.

"I sure did," Paul said. He ruffled his son's hair. "Don't I always do what you tell me?"

"Sometimes," Jeff said seriously.

Bulletproof vests were not mandatory for detectives on the Chicago police force but Paul usually wore his just to be careful. They'd discussed the possibility of his getting shot before. Both boys worried about it.

Paul soothed their fears as best he could. As a single parent, he wanted to assure his sons as much as possible that he would be there for them. Their mother had died giving birth to Jeff.

When Paul finished, Jeff said, "The kids make fun sometimes because you're a cop. I tell them to bug off."

This was one of the hazards of living in a newly upscale neighborhood. A lot of the old ethnic families still remained, but the new condos and town homes were filled with yuppies and their sometimes arrogant kids who looked down on less well-off families.

"Do you want me to talk to the teacher?" Paul asked.

"Nah. It's okay. If it gets bad, I tell them Brian will beat them up." Brian, the star athlete in the neighborhood, had a reputation of toughness and looking out for his brother. Such threats carried weight.

After dinner Paul cleaned up as he prepared to go out. He thought of shaving again, he often did before dates, but Ben, the guy he'd been dating for nearly six months, said he liked the heavy beard. Brian popped his head in his dad's bedroom as Paul was pulling on a gray University of Illinois sweatshirt.

"Dad, can I have Charlette over to study tonight?"

"Charlette, the pretty one from over in the town houses on Harrison?"

"Yeah, you met her last week. Dark hair, nice looking."

"All the girls you date have dark hair and are nice looking."

"Come on, Dad, I need help with my English."

"And Charlette is just the expert you need."

"Well, she gets A's all the time."

"I vaguely recall your report card the past three semesters had A's in English."

"Dad!"

"No dice. If Mrs. Talucci's at home and she agrees, you can study over there, but you have to take your brother with you."

Brian considered his options. He thought of trying whining, but that often backfired into extra sets of chores. Brian said, "Jeff's here, nothing's going to happen while he's around."

"Jeff is not going to start chaperoning you at this stage of his career, much as he might relish the opportunity. Mrs. Talucci or nothing."

Rose Talucci lived next door. Paul loved her. She cared for Jeff every day after school whenever Paul or Brian couldn't be home. She often wound up giving the boys and their dad dinner. This was prearranged on a weekly basis. For several years after it started, she refused all offers of payment. Being neighbors and nearly family precluded even discussing such things. One day Mrs. Talucci couldn't fix a broken porch. Paul offered. Since then he'd done all the repairs on her home and had even done several major renovations. Mrs. Talucci lived on the ground floor by herself. On the second floor lived Mrs. Talucci's two daughters and several distant female cousins. Mrs. Talucci at ninety-one ruled this brood, her main concern being to keep them out of her way and to stay independent. Numerous times she'd confided in Paul that if they weren't family she'd throw them all out. She did her own cooking, cleaning, and shopping as she had for seventy-three years. To her daughters' horror she took the bus on her own throughout the city and suburbs to visit friends and relatives, to shopping-center openings, or to go to anything else that struck her fancy as something new and interesting.

Brian said, "Best deal I'm going to get?"

Paul reached for his black leather jacket. "Yep."

Brian gave a teenage martyr sigh. Paul grabbed his keys and walked toward the door.

Brian said, "You could bring Ben home to stay overnight."

Paul stopped. He searched his son's brown eyes. Seeing seriousness there, he bit back the comment that he didn't know he needed Brian's permission. Ben had stayed over a few times already, often enough to leave a pair of pajama bottoms hanging on a hook in the closet.

"Do you love him?" Brian asked.

Paul said, "Pardon me?"

"Do you love him?"

"Is it important to you that I do?"

"Yeah, kind of. He's nice. I like when he's around. And you're happy when he's with us. You don't smile enough, Dad. You're always so serious."

"I'll tell him you approve," Paul said. "He can come and ask you if he can have my hand in marriage."

"Cool. I'll say yes, but you have to get Mrs. Talucci's permission too."

"No problem. She's been trying to get him to move in with us for ages."

Paul walked down Taylor Street to Ben's garage. Ben had inherited it from his dad a number of years ago. With the influx of new homes and yuppies into the neighborhood the garage did better business than it had in years. New cars needed oil changes and repairs as much as old ones.

The service bay set furthest back from Taylor Street was well lit. Paul strolled back, raised the overhead door and stepped inside.

"We're closed," called a distant gruff voice.

Paul shut the door. Two legs encased in coveralls squirmed under a Porsche.

"It's Paul," he said.

A torso appeared above the legs and then a head. Light brown hair tied back in a pony tail, face and hands smudged with grease, Myra Johnson smiled hello. She often worked late. She had an incredible reputation among the expensive foreign car set who begged her to work on their cars. She prized her private time so she often turned them down. They offered her enormous sums, but she serviced only a select number of people.

"How's the cop biz?" she asked.

"More dead people than I ever thought possible," he said.

"Works that way," she said.

Ben walked in. "Heard voices," he said. He walked up to Paul, and they embraced and kissed.

"You guys are disgusting," Myra said.

"Jealous?" Ben asked.

"No, Bonnie keeps me happy. It's just you guys are always so mushy. You must be in love."

Both men blushed. She eyed them carefully. "Sorry, didn't know you hadn't told each other yet."

The three of them talked for a few minutes. Myra said she had to get finished, and they left her to it. They walked past the parts department to the front offices.

Paul said, "She must be making a ton of money doing overtime."

"We got a new deal," Ben said. "She works for me half the day, then I rent out that space to her for the rest of the time. She charges her customers and gives me a flat fee. I make almost as much from her work as I do from all the rest of the service. She's good."

"I like her," Paul said.

Ben flicked off the lights. He twirled a series of locks to let them out the front. He punched a computer code into a fixture above the door.

"Myra's still here," Paul reminded him.

"She likes to have the alarm on when she's working here alone at night," Ben explained. "She resets it when she's ready to leave." They strolled through the parking lot to Ben's truck.

Ben and Paul had gone through grade school and high school together, but they hadn't noted an attraction at the time. Ben stood an inch or two taller. He wouldn't be called handsome but some might call him rugged. His hair hung a trifle longer than was the usual in the neighborhood. Tonight he wore a white sweater over a blue shirt. These clung to his broad shoulders and tapered into a pair of gray jeans.

In Ben's V-8 engine 1949 red Chevy truck they drove up Lake Shore Drive, past the Loop to the north side. They took Addison past Wrigley Field. They were going to the Music Box Theater to see a showing of *Harold and Maude*. When Ben learned Paul had never seen it, he insisted they go at the first opportunity. That was one reason they were going out tonight, the movie was only playing this once. The other reason was their varied schedules. As a small businessman, Ben rarely had time to get out, and Paul's schedule as a cop was erratic. Their first serious argument a month ago had been over lack of time spent together. They determined that at least once a week they'd make time for each other.

"You wouldn't believe the nut case I had in the shop today," Ben said as they drove up. "Some guy in full leather drag: cap, jacket, pants, maybe even his shirt. He had hair down to his waist in the back. He wore diamond studded sun glasses and rhinestone encrusted boots. He didn't give his name. Just demanded to be treated like royalty."

"What's this guy driving?" Paul asked.

"A $260,000 Bently Continental R that would start but wouldn't keep going. Maybe somebody poured cocaine into the tank. Whatever. He's heard that Myra is the best mechanic in the city and this guy says he only gets the best. No way it could be done. Myra's booked up months in advance and only does emergencies for friends. The guy got really mad and tried to bully Myra. He even pounded his diamond-studded boot on her workbench and shouted threats."

"You didn't throw him out on his ass?"

"I didn't have to. Myra tossed him out on his skinny little butt."

"Physically pitched him out?"

"Yep."

"I'd like to have seen that. What happened to his car?" Paul asked.

"It wouldn't even start anymore so he had to have it towed away."

Paul enjoyed the stories Ben told about the foibles of the patrons of the car repair shop.

They found a parking space just off Southport a block south of the theater. When Ben turned off the engine Paul reached for the door handle.

Ben said, "Hey, cop." He pulled Paul close. Paul enjoyed the strength and warmth, Ben's now-familiar smell of sweat and Old Spice. He felt the bristly mustache as Ben's kiss strengthened. They fooled around until it was time for the show to start.

As Ben had predicted, Paul loved the movie. Afterward in a coffee shop on the other side of Southport, Paul told Ben about the separate conversations with his sons, Jeff's concern about his safety, and Brian's concern about his love life.

Ben said, "I'm glad Brian likes me. I hope Jeff does."

"No problem. He lets you carry him. Lots of people offer, but he only permits a few people to do it. You're okay in his eyes." Jeff liked to be as independent as his birth defect permitted. The boy's standing rule was to 'let me try it, and if I need help I'll ask.' The only people permitted to break this rule were his dad and sometimes Brian. Over the years Paul had learned when the frustration point would come for his son. Being carried was something that took an enormous amount of trust on the boy's part, but he'd taken to Ben from the start.

"You know, Myra was right," Paul said. Ben watched Paul's eyes. He reached for Ben's hand and held it on top of the table. "I do love you."

"Myra's too smart for her own good," Ben said. He patted Paul's hand. "I love you, too."

Ben dropped Paul off at his doorstep. They whispered and kissed briefly before parting.

Paul checked his sleeping sons, Brian lightly snoring, Jeff peacefully quiet. Paul sat on Jeff's bed watching his son sleep for ten minutes before he mounted the steps to his own room.

The next morning Brian made omelets with spinach filling. His eldest son had been on a health kick for two months. Paul didn't want to discourage this voluntary vegetable ingestion, but sighed inaudibly. He'd have to eat it too.

Paul and his sons ate breakfast together every weekday. They rose a half hour early to share at least the one meal together. Last night's supper had been something of a rarity. They used the time in the morning to talk, compare schedules, settle family squabbles. Paul's workday started at eight-thirty, and as much as he tried to stick to a set schedule the amount of overtime required of a detective in Area Ten made this almost impossible. Brian's spring baseball practice began next week and would keep him out until six most nights. Jeff's schedule varied because of his physical therapy. Paul wanted them together at least once a day for a meal one of them cooked. They each took a week and rotated assignments. One cooked, one set the table, one cleaned up. Jeff's meals were, understandably, simple. The kitchen had special chairs, hooks, and pulleys to aid Jeff, although Paul stood ready to help and often assisted Jeff if things got complicated.

At Area Ten headquarters, Turner half listened at roll call.

He leaned against a now-silent radiator. The spring weather had warmed sufficiently to ensure the blessed silence from the aged heating system. The atmosphere in the station would be much improved until the rush of summer humidity drove them nuts.

The building housing Area Ten was south of the River City complex on Wells Street on the southwest rim of Chicago's Loop. The building was as old and crumbling as River City was new and gleaming. Fifteen years ago the department purchased a four-story warehouse scheduled for demolition and decreed it would be a new Area Ten headquarters. To this day, rehabbers occasionally put in appearances. In fits and starts the building had changed from an empty hulking wreck to a people-filled hulking wreck. Wild rumor had it that the conversion from radiators to more modern heating would be done sometime before the end of the century. Maybe they'd get air-conditioning before the beginning of the century after that.

Area Ten ran from Fullerton Avenue on the north to Lake Michigan on the east, south to Fifty-ninth Street, and west to Halsted. It included the wealth of downtown Chicago and North Michigan Avenue, some of the nastiest slums in the city, along with numerous upscale developments. It incorporated four police districts. The cops in the Areas in Chicago handled homicides and any major nonlethal violent crimes. The districts mostly took care of neighborhood patrols and initial responses to incidents.

Turner spent most of roll call leafing through notes from a previous case he was due to testify in at nine-thirty. He enjoyed being on the stand and after years was good at it, but he hated the waiting. The State's attorney had assured him he would be first on the stand this morning. He was testifying in what the other cops in the squad had named the "Doggy Doo Murder." Police often give nicknames to murder cases, a gallows humor that helped them distance themselves from the realities of their jobs. As soon as they'd heard the medical examiner talk about feeding dogs parts of the body to try to get rid of the evidence, somebody had come up with the nickname. Turner thought it stupid, but even he thought of the case by its nickname. Finding the murderer had been simple enough. They'd questioned the neighbors around the alley where pieces of the partly eaten body had been found. They didn't discover anything until they'd expanded their search to a four-block radius. At the first house Turner had gone to with the new perimeter, two Doberman pinschers and a pit bull terrier had nearly flung themselves through the front window of the house.

Even with the dogs on tight leashes, Turner and his partner Fenwick had been reluctant to walk in the door, but the man insisted. He'd let them in, and within fifteen minutes he'd told them the entire story. He'd murdered his wife. She didn't like dogs. She'd given him an ultimatum, her or the animals. Contrary to television murder mysteries, most criminals like to talk. Often you can't shut them up. It's rare that cops have to work hard to solve a mystery. Unless it's gang- or drug-related, the vast majority of the time, the killer knows the victim—husbands, wives, relatives, friends—whom in one moment of passion, they destroy.

The guy with the dogs figured the animals had mangled the body enough so it could never be identified, but since the killing, he'd been consumed by guilt. The guy had wound up pleading not guilty, and although it would probably be a simple case, Turner still had to testify.

Before he left for court he filled Fenwick in on his date last night. Paul's sexual orientation had never been an issue for Fenwick or his wife Madge. Their families had yearly picnics in the summer and get-togethers at holiday times. If Turner was dating someone, he often brought him over.

"Madge wanted me to be sure you brought him along next time you come," Fenwick said. "She hasn't met him yet."

Turner said he would. He checked to make sure no calls had come in, then headed for Twenty-sixth and California. He didn't get away from the criminal courts building until after twelve-thirty. He'd been third on the stand after two dog experts testifying to whether a dog would eat a human. It would. Back at Area Ten he picked up Fenwick and went out to grab some lunch, over most of which Fenwick grumbled. He was on a new diet. Over the years his bulk had increased significantly. His periodic weight regimes ran from the exotic to the marginally nauseous. This week it was lots of steamed vegetables.

As they walked into the squad room Sergeant Felix Poindexter spotted Turner and hurried over.

"A murder at the University of Chicago," Poindexter said. He pointed at them. "The commander wants you guys on it." If a case had the possibility of being politically sensitive or controversial, the commander liked to put Turner and Fenwick in charge. They had a solid reputation for avoiding the pitfalls of swarming reporters and nervous politicos out for their own skin.

"One of the students?" Fenwick asked.

"Professor," Poindexter drew a deep breath, "and alderman."

He didn't need to say any more.

Everybody in Chicago knew Gideon Giles, university professor, liberal alderman, self-appointed devil's advocate, committed gadfly, and headline grabber.

Turner and Fenwick didn't waste time asking what happened. They'd find out all they needed to know at the scene. Turner took the paper with the address from Poindexter, grabbed his regulation blue notebook, and hurried toward the door.

Fenwick snatched the keys to one of the cars and signed it out. Turner was used to Fenwick's race-car tactics. They roared to the on ramp for the Dan Ryan Expressway at Eighteenth Street. The exits in the local lanes crawled by to Fifty-fifth Street. To avoid the traffic, Fenwick rode the shoulder, even on one occasion streaking into the regular lanes to bypass a state cop giving some guy a ticket. Fenwick eased himself onto the campus on University Avenue and down to Fifty-eighth Street. He parked behind a blue-and-white in the cul de sac in the middle of the university quadrangle.

The first golden leaves of spring softened the stark grayness of the university buildings surrounding the quadrangle. Turner found the campus pleasant and soothing amid the bustle of the city. Mike Sanchez, a beat cop Turner knew, waved to them from the doors of a building just to the southwest of the turn around circle. He met them on the steps and walked up with them to the third floor. As they climbed, they spoke about Fenwick's golf game, the Cubs' chances this season, and Sanchez's possibility of making detective. None looked very promising.

As they ascended, the wooden stairs echoed with their footsteps. He led them down a gray-tiled hallway. Most of the office doors they passed remained closed. From a few openings, people gaped. Turner guessed the ones trying to look above it all were professors and the ones looking uncomfortable, slightly embarrassed, or frankly curious to be secretaries, grad students, and assorted hangers-on.

Another uniformed cop stood outside one of the offices.

"You the first ones here?" Turner asked.

"We didn't touch anything," Sanchez said to the unasked question. Turner had worked with Sanchez before, and knew the statement to be true. Sometimes it seemed that cops screwed up a crime scene more than any criminals. What they drilled into you at the academy over and over was: *Don't touch anything.* A few of them actually learned the lesson.

"Didn't much matter, though," Sanchez added.

"Why not?" Turner asked.

Sanchez filled them in on the details.

"I got here about thirty minutes ago." He pointed toward six people sitting in chairs farther down the hall. "Most of them

1 5

had been in the room, were running around spreading the news, or doing their best to be out of control."

"Scene screwed up."

"Pretty much. The guy who gave the alarm doesn't remember what they touched. Half these people have had training in cardiopulmonary resuscitation, mouth-to-mouth resuscitation, and probably the Heimlich maneuver. They tried all of them. The body's probably been moved half a dozen times."

Fenwick said, "Dumb academic shits."

Sanchez said, "Somebody managed to call the campus cops. One of them's around here somewhere. He ran to call us and did nothing to preserve the crime scene. At least a dozen people have been in the room since."

Sanchez had secured the scene as much as possible on arrival, but knew little else of the details.

"How do they know it's murder?" Turner asked.

"Could be suicide, I guess, but I've seen enough corpses," Sanchez said. "I don't think he killed himself."

"Natural causes?" Turner asked.

"You can see for yourself," Sanchez said, "But I'm putting my money on murder."

In Chicago, detectives are taught always to treat any unexplained death as if it were homicide, until and unless there is overwhelming evidence that it is a suicide. Making the mistake of calling a murder a suicide was one quick way to get yourself dumped as a detective. If you erred, you erred on the side of caution—the death was a homicide until proven otherwise.

Turner and Fenwick strode into the office. Dark mahogany paneling halfway up the walls matched that in the hallway. A desk barred their way; also a telephone, papers, cup for coffee with the words NO ONE KNOWS I'M A LESBIAN printed in red on it. A three-by-four-foot calendar took up the space on the wall to the right of the desk. Immediately behind the desk, against a back wall, a table neatly filled with stacks of papers, above the table an enormous map of the Fifth Ward, which included the

University and stretched along the lake from Fifty-third Street on the North to Seventy-ninth Street on the south with its furthest west boundary irregularly drawn, but never going beyond Cottage Grove. The boundaries included the area for the 1893 Columbian Exposition, and large parts of the old South Shore neighborhood, once heavily Jewish, now mostly black.

The Fifth Ward had a long tradition of maverick politics and politicians, often pains in the ass to the old Democratic machine. The most famous graduate of the ward was Paul Douglas, slated by the Democrats for the United States Senate in 1948, his victory was almost as much of a surprise as Truman's. The Democratic machine had run him for Senate because, as an independent, he caused them too much trouble in the City Council.

Gideon Giles came out of the same tradition, only more so. The first University of Chicago professor to be elected to the City Council. He never let pass an opportunity to tweak the noses of regular Democrats. The machine may not have been what it once was, but it knew how to handle political outsiders. They ignored him. Giles could call for investigations, denounce unliberal actions, and decry the evil of the right wing, but not a resolution, proposal, or idea of his ever received more than a handful of votes in the City Council.

Giles participated in everything. If there was a save the whales, antinuclear energy, pro-choice, antidiscrimination, or any kind of march, sit-in, or protest, he was there, somehow managing to worm his way in front of the cameras. Now the media sought him out for the quick interview, the easy quote.

The desk and back table took up seven-eighths of the room. A door to the left led to an inner office.

From the outer office Turner saw the body, clothes ripped, face distorted, laying faceup on the floor, head toward the door.

T W O

Both cops stood silently just inside the doorway. The room smelled of old books and vomit. Turner blocked the smell from his mind. He'd sensed worse at more horrific scenes. From long practice they let their eyes examine everything in the room first. One of the truisms of cop lore is that the murderer always leaves a sign of his presence. As screwed up as this crime scene obviously was, they needed to note every detail they saw.

"Triple fuck," Fenwick said. Turner knew that Fenwick's expletive was the highest rating anyone or anything could get in his partner's classification system. Usually Fenwick reserved this sacred category for inept Bears quarterbacks when they threw game-losing interceptions, or Cubs pitchers who walked in winning runs. The system proceeded through three levels of "shit" to the highest "fuck" category. This crime scene certainly rated the most negative classification.

Turner and Fenwick pulled out pens and began making notes starting with the time of the call, the unit numbers of the cops, and the time of their arrival. Turner did a quick sketch of the outer office and the perspective of the body. He'd have pictures of all this later, but he wanted his own memories. He noted items on the desk, walls, and floor. Finished he slowly walked toward the corpse.

He seethed with anger as he did this. One thing a detective hates is a contaminated crime scene. This one looked like a herd of buffaloes had been through it. You got your feel for a crime from what you saw, and what Turner saw wasn't the crime but the aftermath of well-intentioned people trying to help. His anger cooled when he realized the horror they must have gone through trying to save the dying man.

As Turner approached the corpse, he was barely aware of the process his mind whirled through asking the myriad of questions that viewing of hundreds of crime scenes had engrained on his mind. Why did the person die here? How? He was already drawing his picture of this room. No blood trail. From the doorway he stared at the body, searching for meaning and sense. Jewelry still on. Pockets not turned inside out. The room was strewn with papers. Careful not to disturb any of them, Turner eased around the room. Where was the body before the rescuers got there? Did the killer come back as part of that group? Did the murderer leave glaring mistakes behind? In more than ninety percent of the cases, this was the saving grace for the cop, the killer's tendency toward making a dumb mistake.

Turner spent fifteen minutes filling his notebook with observations and details. A blue cup in back of the desk contained the dregs of a vile-smelling greenish liquid. An electronic juicer on the table near the door had remnants of a similar fluid.

The trash can proved to be the source of the vile odors. Vomit flecked tissues, remnants of the frantic efforts to help the dying man, half filled the receptacle. Turner would keep his notes. The schematic drawing Fenwick was working on would be for the official file.

Turner gazed at the body. Giles hardly looked to be at rest. The body was on its back, muscles rigid in convulsion, the eyes wide open, and an extreme facial grimace. He touched the body. Rigor already set in.

Fred Nokosinski, the bearded dwarf who took crime scene pictures, stood in the doorway holding his Canon AI-1s. "Ready for pictures?" he asked.

"Start in the outer room," Turner said. "Make sure you get the positions of all the papers there and in here."

Fred jerked his thumb over his shoulder, "You got visitors."

"What the hell?" Fenwick said. He looked through the doorway. He saw the case sergeant, the commander of the local police district, and a cop from the superintendent's office he recognized but whose name he didn't remember.

"Nuts," Turner muttered. He and Fenwick hurried to the door of the outer office. As detective in charge of the crime scene, Turner knew that technically he had more power than any cop in the city in these few square feet. That didn't stop the brass in a case like this from trying to trample over every square inch of territory.

Fenwick planted his large bulk in front of the mass of brass and said, "I'll give you all you need."

Turner turned on his heel and returned to the body.

He found Fred Nokosinski on top of a nicked-up wooden chair, focusing his camera down on the body.

Sam Franklin, head of the crime lab unit, entered the room. His sharp eyes took in the scene, barely glancing at the body. He snorted in derision. "Stupid politicians will go off like demented fire alarms over this."

Turner nodded.

"You ready for us?" Franklin asked.

Turner scanned the room carefully. "I want to examine the

papers. That'll take a while. I'll handle them as little as possible and send them along."

Franklin directed his minions in their tasks. Dusting for fingerprints, vacuuming the floor—contents to be sifted later, doing everything delicately so that every bit of human existence in the room could be carefully examined later.

The space from which Gideon Giles ruled his domain was about ten by ten. Posters advocating his favorite causes filled the walls. A bulletin board to the right of the door covered the entire wall, floor to ceiling. It contained business cards, a mass of eight-and-a-half by eleven multihued circulars and press releases announcing specific dates and times for meetings of the groups advertised around the room. Next to a notice for the Flat-Earth Society was a flyer giving the time for a meeting of ACT-UP.

Turner waited for the technical people to finish. The medical examiner came in fifteen minutes after the crime lab people started. He scrutinized the body. He spoke as he worked the room at large. "Wasn't stabbed or shot." A gray-haired man whom Turner didn't like, the medical examiner mumbled to himself as he unbuttoned, prodded, and pushed at the body. He examined the neck carefully. "Wasn't strangled."

Turner resisted the impulse to give his opinion of what killed Giles. He knew from experience that if he spoke, he'd get an officious lecture.

The ME mumbled. "Probably poison."

Turner had seen enough murders to have made this guess forty-five minutes ago, but he kept quiet. The ME had to earn his paycheck too.

Turner had examined the small refrigerator in the corner of the room nearest the window. He used his pen wedged around the handle to open the door. Inside he'd found six bottles. Three were filled with health-food juices with safety seals intact. The other three had no labels and no safety seals. Green liquid with orange flecks in it filled two of these to the brim. One was half full. He called Sam Franklin over. With exquisite care, the two of them pulled the half full bottle out of the refrigerator and removed its cap.

"Smells vile," Franklin said.

"Better take special care of everything in the refrigerator," Turner said.

Franklin agreed. "You see the juicer on the table by the door?"

"Take it with you," Turner said.

Turner followed the medical examiner out of the room. Fenwick stood at the open doorway talking to the commander of Area Ten. He was a tall black man with snow-white hair. The commander hadn't tried to enter the room, and Tuner knew he wouldn't. He saw the other brass out in the hallway.

Fenwick caught Turner's look. "I was lucky to keep them out. I almost had to tackle the guy from the superintendent's office."

"Do it if you have to," the commander said. "This is going to be tough enough as it is. What have you got?"

"ME said poison," Turner said. "I agree. No food in evidence, but we've got a cup on the desk with residue in it. Could have come from the juice container in the refrigerator. Probably in the drink. We've got to figure out how the killer put it there. He or she had to risk being recognized, if it was administered here. Depends on the kind of poison."

"Could it have been suicide?" the commander asked.

"Possible," Turner said, "but I haven't seen a note. We'll be checking it."

"Anything else yet?" the commander asked.

"Just starting to question the locals. Going to take a while," Turner told him.

"Lots of press and public attention on this one," the commander said.

22

"Usual with this kind of thing," Turner said.

The commander sighed. "More than usual. I can't believe how many calls I've gotten from aldermen worried about their sacred persons." He rubbed a hand across his face. "I'll try to keep the pressure off you guys as best I can, but it would sure as hell help if you came up with a killer as soon as possible."

He didn't comment further on their investigation or try to make suggestions. He trusted Turner and Fenwick to do what was right. They had a 95 percent conviction rate; they knew how to make an arrest and knew what to do to make it stick. The commander wished them luck and strolled over to the cops from downtown. Fenwick and Turner returned to the outer office.

Turner examined the massive oak desk itself, then shifted carefully through the papers on top. No suicide note. An appointment calendar lay on the upper right-hand corner of the desk. Giles had had a university committee meeting later that day but nothing else. With the tip of his pen Turner turned over the leaf to Monday. The previous evening Giles had met with a group called Friends of the Furred and Finny. Turner checked the past weeks and the next few. He wrote down the names of all the groups and people. The most appointments he'd had in a day was six. A few days had nothing. He found several phone messages and took down the names and numbers on them.

Sam Franklin brought in two mugs encased in large plastic bags. Turner glanced in both of them.

"These are all we found in the room," Franklin said. He pointed to a dark-blue one. "Found this on the floor behind the desk. We'll find traces on the inside. Got to be poison in it."

"That's my guess," Turner said.

He got Sanchez to bring in each of the witnesses from the hall one by one. They started with the person who sounded the alarm. They talked in the outer office. The witness in one of the chairs, Fenwick leaning on the table in the back, Turner sitting on the edge of the desk.

Clark Burke was a student at the university. Five-foot-six, maybe all of 120 pounds, blond hair standing out straight from the top of his head an inch, cut short on the sides. He wore a button-down white shirt, black Z. Cavaricci pants with the label at the zipper, and black athletic shoes. Turner noted Burke's fingertips were red, and the nails chewed down. Burke spoke in a surprisingly deep and mellow voice. Most of the time his hands hung nearly motionless on the chair arms, except for occasional forays to his mouth, where a fingernail got chewed.

They found out he was a student temp who substituted for different departments when secretaries called in sick or were out on vacation. He answered phones, took messages, and did some typing. He was a sophomore at the university, majoring in English.

Turner observed that Burke's eyes made surreptitious glances at Turner's crotch.

Turner asked, "Could you tell us what happened?"

"I'm a little shook up. I don't know what you want me to say." Burke chewed on a nail.

"Start at the beginning," Turner suggested. "Tell us what you did today."

"I've worked in this department a couple times before, never for Mr. Giles until this week. His regular secretary is on vacation. The head of the department, Mr. Sorenson, always asks for me when one of the secretaries is out. I know most of the members of the department."

"How well did you know Mr. Giles?" Turner asked.

"A little. I knew who he was by sight. Did somebody really poison him?"

Fenwick asked, "How did you know he was poisoned?"

"That's what people in the hall said. I thought he was having a heart attack."

"How was he to work for the past two days?" Turner asked.

"Yesterday, Monday, I only saw him for a few minutes. He gave me a bunch of stuff to type. This morning he came in and asked how I was doing on the typing. I still had ten pages to do. He didn't say much else."

"It would help if you could give us as many details about today as possible," Turner said. "Anything you could remember might be important."

Burke chewed on a nail for a minute, then noticed he was doing it. "Nervous habit," he muttered. He held one hand with the other in his lap. He said, "I got here at nine. That's the usual starting time. For the first couple hours I was here by myself. I just answered the phone and typed."

"How many calls were there?" Fenwick asked.

"Only a few. I don't remember the messages. I put them on his desk."

"Did people from other offices come in?"

Burke thought. "A few people put their heads in the door and asked for Gwendolen, the regular secretary, but nobody came in for Giles. He came in about eleven-thirty. I told him about the messages. He gave me a couple more things to type. I can only do fifty words a minute so it takes me quite a while to get anything done. The biggest thing was a manuscript for an article."

"What was the manuscript about?" Fenwick asked.

" 'Mythos in Chaucer's *Troilus*: A Post-Structural Analysis.' "

"What the hell does that mean?" Fenwick asked.

Burke shrugged.

"Did you see him after he gave you the work?"

Burke said, "He came out once near noon and told me I could go to lunch and not worry about how long I took. He did the same thing yesterday. I think he was trying to be nice. I took an hour. We usually take only half that."

Turner noted Burke's demeanor and mannerisms while the

nineteen-year-old talked. Burke looked him in the eye when he answered; he seemed to be thinking carefully about his answers rather than cautiously. Burke told them that no one came in to see Giles after the professor showed up for work.

"You leave anytime during the morning?" Turner asked.

"Just for a break around ten. I was gone maybe fifteen minutes. Then a few minutes after Giles got here, I went down to go to the john."

"How long were you gone then?" Turner asked.

"Maybe five minutes. I had to use the washroom on the second floor. I couldn't find the key to the one on this floor."

Turner asked, "What happened when you got back from lunch?"

"I finished typing some letters and took them in to him."

"What were they about?" Turner asked.

"Mostly to magazines about articles he planned to write. I think he was a little surprised to see me."

"Did you notice what he was drinking?" Turner asked.

"I saw his mug. I don't know what was in it. Don't know where he got it."

"Why do you think he was surprised that you came back?" Turner asked.

"Some of the temps try to take advantage. Most of them, if they got told to take as long as they want, they'd take advantage and not show up for a couple hours. If the temp agency caught them, they could be in trouble. I don't want to risk losing this job."

"How did he seem when you talked to him?" Fenwick asked.

"Well, I can't compare it to how he was normally, because I'd never talked to him until this week, but he seemed kind of rattled and busy."

Turner watched the blues eyes searching his. He saw that Burke rubbed his hands on his pants legs, probably sweating. Did Burke realize he was a suspect in a murder case? Nervous at being questioned by the police, probably for the first time in his life? Certainly scared at what had happened.

"What made you think he was rattled and busy?" Fenwick asked.

"Well, he was polite mostly, but gruff, like, thank you and get out I'm busy. We temps are used to that. Most people think we're dirt, but it's a good way to make money to get through college."

"Did anyone come in after you left?" Turner asked.

"Nope."

"Then what happened?" Fenwick asked.

"Well, I sat down here at the computer. I was several pages into a manuscript, the Chaucer article, when I heard a thump from the room next door. I didn't pay much attention, but then I heard horrible gasping and more thumps."

Burke stood up, jammed his hands in his pants pockets, and walked to the doorway to the hall. He glanced left and right then turned back to the two cops, crossing his arms and leaning a shoulder against the door jamb. He spoke softly but without hesitation. "I rushed into the room. I saw him on the floor. I ran to him. He gasped a few more times. I ran to the drinking fountain down the hall to get him some water. I ran back in. He was still breathing. I shouted for help. He started to throw up and have some sort of convulsions. It was awful." He drew several deep breaths. "People came running. I'm not sure who or how many. I was pretty shook up. I do remember dialing nine-one-one."

Burke slowly walked back to the chair and sat down gingerly. He gulped. "I've never watched somebody die."

His eyes found Turner's. The cop returned the gaze, saw a misty-eyed confusion and something else in the lingering look he wasn't sure of. Burke couldn't tell them any more. They'd check into his background and story later.

At this moment two paramedics carried the body bag out. Turner watched Burke turn stark white. Turner told the kid he could go. Burke, his color still bad, managed to gasp, "Are my parents going to find out about this?"

Turner said, "At the moment we don't plan on calling them. Are they a problem? Should we call them?"

"My parents are going to be worried," he said. "My dad especially didn't want me to come to Chicago."

"How's that?" Turner asked.

"I'm from Chatsworth, Iowa. A town near the left end of nowhere. They still think the people in Chicago carry machine guns and shoot each other like in Prohibition times. I was glad to get away."

"Trouble at home?" Turner asked.

"Don't get me wrong," Burke said, "I love my mom and dad. It's just they aren't used to the big city. I'd never been able to go here if I hadn't gotten a big scholarship. I still have to work. Farming is tough in the part of Iowa I'm from. If they hear I'm involved in a murder, they could get real upset. I don't want to go back."

Turner tried to be reassuring while making no commitments about who he would or wouldn't tell.

The next person to be interviewed was Atherton Sorenson, head of the English department. Sorenson had a fringe of white hair around a bald scalp. He wore a Ban-Lon shirt on a sloped shouldered frame and khaki pants with a belt pulled to the last loop on a slightly thickened waist. He stepped a foot inside the door and stopped.

Sorenson spoke in a mellifluous baritone. With his hands he made wide solemn gestures. Turner could see him pontificating in front of groups of graduate students, staring back with glazed expressions. Sorenson didn't wait to be asked a question, but began orating at them unbidden. "Politics. This is the result of getting involved in the muck. I told Giles again and again, it was not seemly for him to be involved with that filth. I wanted him to take a leave of absence, and then when he won that battle, I wanted him to quit, but the higher-ups in the university wouldn't listen. They should have."

Turner could easily imagine the man, at a later, more seemly time, trying to score points with his peers about how right he'd been about that Gideon Giles.

Fenwick said, "Tell us where you were from noon to one-thirty today."

Sorenson looked startled at Fenwick's tone. Turner had worked with his partner long enough to distinguish between his normal abruptness and his genuine dislike for someone. This was the latter. Turner didn't care for Sorenson either, but he didn't want to turn off these people now, but he also didn't mind Fenwick's gruffness. It might shake something loose from a guilty person.

"We need everyone's movements on this floor," Turner said. "Someone might have seen the killer."

Sorenson took this a little better. He swept to the chair and settled his expansive rear end onto its wood. He placed a finger against the right side of his head and stared at the ceiling. He said, "I lunched at the Quadrangle Club as I always do. I remember today's discussion was about the relation between sunlight on hawthorn leaves in Proust and darkness and light in *Timon of Athens*. I always try to have a topic for my colleagues to discuss at the table." He lowered his head to look at them. "I don't suppose you read Proust?"

Fenwick growled. Sorenson raised an eyebrow at him. Turner asked, "Who did you have lunch with?"

"A young instructor, James Everly, the head of the Philosophy department, Bertram Elston, and one or two visitors from the Sorbonne. I don't remember their names. They aren't important, are they?"

"Was Giles there?"

"No. He didn't join us today."

"Did he usually?" Turner asked.

"Not often. I'd say a quarter of the time. When he became alderman, he took part in far fewer activities connected to the University."

"What time did you finish?" Turner asked.

"Around one. I returned to my office and stayed there the whole time. You can ask my secretary. She'll vouch for me."

Turner asked about relationships between faculty members.

"You mean did he have any enemies?" Sorenson asked.

"Anything you can tell us about how he got along with his colleagues."

Sorenson settled himself back in the chair this time, leaning a finger of his left hand against his head and staring at the ceiling. "Well, he didn't really get along with us at all. Not in the sense that he had enemies, but he was above us all. He had that more-committed-than-thou attitude, which I thought disappeared with the sixties. You've seen the posters in his office. He didn't meet a cause he didn't embrace." Sorenson explained that in terms of departmental politics, Giles was not an important factor, and that Giles stayed on at the university so he'd have a political base. "It looked good on his credentials. A legitimate profession as opposed to alderman in this city." Turner thought Sorenson made the job of alderman sound worse than that of a rat collector.

"Did he seem depressed to you lately?" Turner asked.

"You mean was he suicidal? Definitely not. Man had an ego to match Lear in Act I."

They asked about Giles's background.

He'd had excellent credentials. Graduated from the University, did post-graduate work there and at Stanford. He'd become a full professor the year before he'd branched out into politics. This was about ten years ago.

"Did he always do causes?" Turner asked.

"No. When he got here, he was quite the subservient young man. Minded his manners. Made a good impression on everyone. Careful in his opinions on academic matters. He rarely took a chance in the research he published, but it was always solidly reasoned." Giles had gotten heavily into causes the year after he got tenure, had become quite obnoxious, insisting the department take absurd positions. "He wanted to declare the department a nuclear-free zone. I thought he might be losing his mind. Nobody was going to build a nuclear power plant on this university campus. Some professors become eccentric in their old age, but Giles went balmy on us early."

"Could you get rid of him?" Fenwick asked.

Sorenson gaped at him, pointed a finger, breathed deeply and said, "Tenure laws are inviolate. I'm sure you're not suggesting we make the life of a professor subject to the whims of fortune."

Fenwick growled, "No enemies?"

"None," Sorenson said quickly. Turner thought his majesty might be a little intimidated by Fenwick, and he enjoyed watching it, but they still had to get any information out of him they could.

"Do you know if Giles had any habits about what he drank or ate here at the University?" Turner asked.

"I haven't the faintest notion," Sorenson said.

"Did you see anybody or anything unusual at any time today? Any strangers walking through the building?" Turner asked.

Sorenson thought a moment, then shook his head no.

"Notice any change in Giles lately? Unusually nervous or tense?"

Another elegant shake of the head.

"Did he have a habit of drinking one particular thing in his office every day?" Turner asked.

"You can ask his secretary Gwendolen when she returns from vacation. Now that I think about it, I vaguely recall he tried to eat healthy things. Perhaps drank carrot juice and such nonsense."

They let him go.

Fenwick said, "Stupid, overintellectual. Bet he doesn't know shit about the real world."

Turner heard shouting coming from the hallway outside.

"I'll check it out," Fenwick said.

Moments later the bulky cop flew backwards through the doorway, landing with his back against a poster that ripped and fell off the wall.

Turner jumped up. A tall black woman stood in the doorway. She sneered at Fenwick, then stepped aside. A pale woman staggered into the room. She wore a velvet dress, gold-flecked tulle scarf, and clutched Alain Mikli sunglasses in one hand.

"Where is he?" she gasped.

Sanchez appeared at the door. "Sorry, Paul. They busted past us. Want me to get rid of them?"

"I'll do it." Fenwick marched toward her.

Turner held up a hand. "Who are . . . ?"

The starkly pale woman said, "I'm Laura Gideon Giles." She pointed to the black woman. "Lilac called me at work. She said something terrible had happened. She told me my husband is, is . . ."

Laura Giles took a deep breath and drew herself up very straight. Her violet eyes searched theirs for several moments. She said, "I think I would like to sit down."

Turner hated dealing with the families of the victims, especially if he was the one who had to break the news. He'd been spared that difficulty this time.

They helped Laura Giles to a chair. Dry-eyed and dazed, she whispered, "What happened?"

Turner told her as much as they knew.

After he finished she muttered, "I don't believe it. This morning we talked about remodeling our cottage in Michigan. It was one of his favorite places, and we'd just decided to fix it up. I can't believe we'll never . . . I don't know what to do."

"We know this is a difficult time, Mrs. Giles, but if you

could answer a few questions, it might help us find your husband's killer."

"Murdered," she said.

She rummaged in her purse and pulled out a pack of Virginia Slims and some matches. Fenwick gave her a styrofoam cup with a layer of coffee in the bottom to use as an ashtray.

"Can we get you something?" Turner asked.

She blew smoke out through her nostrils. "A cup of tea, please." Lilac left, returning a few minutes later with a steaming cup. She remained standing in the doorway.

Laura Giles took a large gulp of the hot liquid, shut her eyes, and breathed the vapors. She put the cup down, took another long drag on her cigarette, missed the ashtray with a flick of ash, and turned to stare up at Turner.

"A few questions please, Mrs. Giles," Turner said.

Her body shook for several moments. She stabbed the cigarette into the cup. Turner heard it sizzle. She crossed her arms tightly over her chest, looked up, and said, "I'll help any way I can to find his murderer."

Turner asked for background on Giles's life, who might have grudges from years ago, who might not like him now.

Mrs. Giles explained that she and her husband had met in graduate school at Stanford University. She majored in business law and he in English and political science. They'd dated for three years during graduate school, then moved together to Southern California. While Gideon worked on his Ph.D. in English, she attended USC for her M.B.A.

"We were so broke those years. We had a million fights about money. We threatened to call it quits nearly every week. He just had no head for money. Give him a credit card and he went nuts. I had to take them all away."

"But you got married eventually," Turner said.

"We went into therapy for a year together and resolved our differences. We always loved each other. We just had a lot of growing up to do."

After receiving their degrees, they'd worked together for several years on projects to help the homeless in Southern California.

"Those were the happiest times of our lives. We felt committed. We knew our work was paying off. We could see results. Shelters built. Men and women placed in homes."

She'd gotten a business offer from an old college friend. They'd moved to Chicago. Gideon continued his work with the homeless. Laura Giles prospered in business. Gideon eventually landed the job at the University of Chicago.

As far as she knew, he had no enemies from before the time she met him. "After he got the job at the University, we moved to Hyde Park. He got involved in the community, moved up the ranks in the department. People in higher education have all kinds of petty quarrels. Who doesn't at work? And some of them became jealous when the community began pushing him for alderman."

"Who was jealous?" Turner asked.

"Sorenson, the head of the department, for one. I don't really remember the names now." She said that Giles had made enemies as his notoriety grew and his ability to grab the attention of reporters expanded. "People didn't like it, that this articulate, good man could promote programs and causes so well."

Fenwick said, "I thought not one of his bills ever got passed in the city council."

"There are other ways to exercise influence," she said. "Just being an alderman in this city gives you some clout. We'd been in enough causes over the years to know that you don't always succeed by just getting votes."

"Any political enemies?" Turner asked.

"Not really. He fought with people, but he was always professional about it. They understood each other. The only one who held a grudge of any kind was the man he replaced as ward committeeman."

"Who was that?" Turner asked.

"That awful Mike McGee."

Turner didn't recognize the name. "Tell me about him."

"McGee had this more-committed-than-thou attitude. He'd supported lots of causes but never seemed to get anything accomplished for any of them. His reform candidates always seemed to lose. My husband found out he'd been robbing the organizations that trusted him. Siphoning off funds."

"What happened?" Turner asked.

"Gideon talked to him privately. Offered him a deal that if he quit, he wouldn't report him. McGee refused, so my husband defeated him in the election."

They'd have to interview McGee.

"How about neighbors?" Turner asked. "Any problems there?"

"No. We had little contact with them. Our lives were too busy."

Still they'd have to visit the neighbors.

"Did he eat or drink anything specific every day. A habit people might have been aware of?" Turner asked.

"We usually had coffee together at home in the morning. I know he was into health foods. He brought his own vegetables and juices for his own concoctions. He never made them at home. Why is that important?"

"We think something he drank was poisoned," Turner said.

"Oh." She lit another cigarette and smoked in silence, staring at the walls. A few tears escaped from the corners of her eyes. She fished a lace handkerchief out of her purse and dabbed her eyes, but the tears became a flow. She buried her face in the hanky. The African-American woman put her arms around her. Laura Giles crumbled into the embrace and cried softly.

A few minutes later the two women left, leaning heavily on each other. Turner's memory of the night his wife died was dim. He remembered being numb. Knew he cried in his best friend's arms.

"Who was the African-American woman?" Turner asked Sanchez.

"One of the members of the department, Lilac Ostergard," Sanchez said. "Folks out here say she's Mrs. Giles's best friend."

They spent the next hour interviewing seven other people, those who'd rushed in to help, others in the department. Mostly they confirmed what they'd learned already. All of them showed varying degrees of being upset at the loss of a co-worker. None of them had seen any strangers or anyone suspicious lurking in the halls.

Turner felt a cop's twinge of suspicion about two of the faculty members. Sure they weren't telling the truth, and his instinct told him to check them out. Most of the time believing an instinct wasn't going to get him far in court, but he trusted it enough to follow it up.

The first was Darcy Worthington, a blond-haired man in his late forties, about the same age as Giles, he spoke with a New England accent.

In response to their questioning, he'd told them that years ago he and Giles had been best friends. "We started the same year," Worthington said. "We got together with our wives often, but I want to make sure I tell you before the gossips around here do. We had a falling out over his political activities."

"You disagree with him philosophically?" Turner asked.

"Not too much, no. We fought because I discovered he was the most ruthlessly ambitious person I'd ever met. I didn't see that side of him until he decided to run for office. Winning consumed him." He shook his head. "I regretted the loss of the friendship. We never really quarreled openly. I just let the friendship drift and stopped responding to him."

When he left, Turner said, "I want to check him out more."

Fenwick said, "I wouldn't trust him as far as I could pound his butt into the pavement."

The other suspicious person was Otto Kempe. Otto was a roly-poly man, Turner guessed to be in his mid forties. He mopped his forehead with an enormous starched white handkerchief after every other sentence.

"I heard the cries for help," he said. "I rushed over. My office is across the hall. It was a mad whirl of people. I was frightened, but I took CPR many years ago, before it became fashionable. I tried to revive him. People were shouting and screaming. Every time someone yelled, he spasmed." Kempe puffed breaths out for several minutes. After a thorough face wipe, he continued, "He died in my arms. It was awful. It was ghastly. I never want to go through something like that again."

They let him compose himself for several minutes.

They asked him a few more questions. Like everyone else, he hadn't seen any strangers, nor had he seen Giles.

"How'd he get along with people in the department?" Turner asked.

"We're academics, dedicated to research. We try to care about ideas, not personalities. I like to think I did that most of the time. People might tell you that Giles and I took opposite sides on esoteric academic issues. Our Chaucer essays were wonders to behold. I thought of it as a friendly rivalry of a good sort."

Kempe left a few minutes later.

"Him I don't like," Fenwick said. "Stupid hanky."

They walked back to the inner office to begin checking through all the papers. Turner tried to avoid getting the remnants of fingerprint powder all over his clothes.

"Killer must have had a hell of nerve," Fenwick said. "Might have been recognized coming in here. Could have been surprised by Burke coming back early."

"Or the person could have come in days before," Turner said, "placed the poison in the juice and waited for him to drink it, but you're right. He or she had to risk being recognized."

They spent the next two hours going through every piece of paper in Gideon Giles's office. They confirmed Burke's story about messages. They found countless letters from causes asking for support. They switched on the computer and ran through seven of the twenty-eight computer discs. Near five o'clock, Sanchez stuck his head in.

The beat cop said, "I got two people out here. One says he's from the University press office and the other claims she's a representative of the University administration."

Turner and Fenwick put up with a mild dose of administrative 'Let's involve the university in as little scandal as possible.' Turner let them indulge in their bureaucratic skittishness and then ushered them out the door.

"We're not going to finish this anytime soon," Fenwick said after he returned from hustling them out of the office. "Let's leave a guard and get something to eat."

They walked over to Hutchinson Commons and grabbed a couple of sandwiches and some coffee and sat in the dark wood-panelled dining hall. Fenwick gazed at the portraits staring down at them and asked, "Who are all the old farts?"

Turner shrugged. He knew Fenwick rarely expected answers to impossible questions.

At the far end of the dining hall, Turner noticed Clark Burke sitting with a handsome young man who had a large green book bag on the table next to him. He watched curiously as the two engaged in intent conversation. Turner nudged Fenwick and pointed. The two cops watched the students for a few minutes.

"I think the kid's gay," Fenwick said.

"I agree," Turner replied, "but I don't think that little snippet of information is going to get us any closer to who killed Gideon Giles."

Turner wanted to talk to some of the people in Giles's Fifth Ward organization. He suggested they leave the papers in

Giles's office until later; they'd gone over most of the important ones.

"I want to try and see some of these campaign people today," Turner said. He'd taken a blank piece of the campaign stationery with the office address on it.

They drove to Fifty-seventh and Dorchester. A lone figure stared out the window when they walked into the headquarters. The office was one of several in a one-story building on the north side of the street.

The decorations on the walls repeated the scheme in Giles's office. Poster after poster of causes lined every surface. Turner saw one of Che Guevara tucked in a corner of a rear wall.

The man staring out the window appeared to be in his mid thirties. He didn't acknowledge their presence until they stood directly in front of him. He wore gold-rimmed glasses, had short-cropped hair, and wore a white t-shirt with the words YOU GOTTA BELIEVE in faded blue letters across the chest.

He let his eyes rove to the two of them and said, "Everybody's gone. The alderman's dead."

They showed their stars and identified themselves. The man blinked and sighed. He told them his name was Frank Ricken.

"Where'd everybody go?" Fenwick asked.

"Press conference." Ricken leaned back in the chair. "That's what this office specialized in. Press conferences. We lived to get him on TV. I've got the numbers of all the important television and radio contacts memorized. We knew media and manipulated them. First-name basis with all the local reporters in the city. And all we got is murder. That's how it's always been. If you get an effective liberal, kill him."

Fenwick asked, "You think a conservative killed him?"

"The right wing in this country has destroyed every liberal cause, with vicious lies, distortions, every dirty trick in the book. They'd easily resort to murder. There's lots of right-wing crazies out there."

"What were you in the organization?" Fenwick asked.

"Campaign chairperson, specializing in press relations. Not the spokesperson. We had somebody in a gray suit and tie to make the announcements to the press. People like to see "respectable" spokespersons. I controlled contacts."

"How come you're here if there's a press conference somewhere else?"

"What's the point? The cause is lost. It always is."

Turner asked, "Did he get any specific threats lately, anybody he annoyed more than anyone else?"

"The mayor of the city of Chicago and the other forty-nine alderman. They all hated him."

"Somebody specific. Did he mention any new problems? Something that might have come up recently."

"Not to me. And he'd have told me. We were close."

They asked how the alderman's organization functioned.

Ricken said, "Giles very much believed in lack of structure. If somebody came in and they had a cause, they worked on it. We had two people who did nothing but work on the problems in Central America."

"Isn't that a kind of unusual project for a Chicago alderman?" Fenwick asked.

"All causes were welcome here. Gideon Giles truly believed in giving his all to the helpless, the hopeless, and the homeless."

Fenwick said, "We need to seal the office off, examine the files."

Ricken said, "I can authorize that. I have access to everything in the office."

Turner said, "Could you show us around, explain what we're looking at? I'm sure you want to help us find who killed him. You never know what might be significant."

Ricken led them into an inner office. It was a shabby duplicate of the professor's office, more posters for more causes filling the walls. Pamphlets stacked on tables crammed against each wall. A desk strewn with paraphernalia sat in the middle of the room.

Ricken explained the system, then excused himself, and the cops got to work. Half an hour later, Fenwick walked out to see about some coffee. He stuck his head back in the office. "That Ricken guy's gone."

Turner joined him in the outer office. "I don't like that," Turner said.

"He got spooked and ran," Fenwick said.

Turner shrugged. "We can find him later. Why not get a couple beat cops over here and seal the place off? We should have done that earlier."

They spent another hour going through the office, but found nothing that might have indicated a murderer. They ducked under the DO NOT CROSS police ribbon and were saying good night to the beat cop on duty when a woman in her fifties approached them. She wore a gray skirt and blue sweater, her gray-flecked hair hung to her shoulders. She saw them, the police barrier, and said, "I'm Mable Ashcroft, the alderman's chief assistant, and you are?"

Turner and Fenwick identified themselves.

Ashcroft said, "Are we going to be able to get our personal items from inside?"

Turner watched her carefully in the late spring afternoon. The air was cool and a light breeze blew off the lake. Pathetic dribs of water leaked from the remnants of a few snowdrifts. Ashcroft had red-rimmed eyes and a worried expression. Turner said, "Why don't we go inside and talk?"

They sat near the front window at a table crammed with papers, boxes, and equipment. Fenwick shoved several phones and piles of papers out of the way.

Turner asked, "Who's Frank Ricken?"

Ashcroft drew her hand to her throat, her eyes widened. "Was he here?"

"He was the only one here when we arrived," Turner said.

"He's not supposed to be here. He got fired last week."

She told them about the internal bickering that went on in the ward office. One faction after another pushed one cause after the other. Giles supported all of them, but each faction lobbied for more and more of his time. A tear rolled down her cheek. "He genuinely tried to help people. He was always torn, trying to do so much. He always said there wasn't enough time to help all those who needed it."

"Why was Ricken fired?" Turner asked.

"Frank always tried too hard. His cause was saving the wetlands. Not a big issue in this ward. He'd get furious if we didn't care as much as he wanted us to. Gideon helped as much as he could, but Frank was never satisfied." The alderman had a huge meeting every Saturday with representatives of all the different causes, trying to get them to work together or form coalitions. "Frank took up more and more time at the meetings. He became more and more strident."

"Do all the people from the causes get jobs in the ward office?" Turner asked.

"No, it was the other way around. If you worked for the alderman, you were encouraged to get involved in a cause."

"Did Graham ever fight with Giles publicly?" Turner asked.

"At the last meeting he threatened all of us. Told us we'd be sorry for not listening to him. Maybe this is what he meant."

She retrieved Ricken's address for them. They asked about other possible conflicts.

Ashcroft said, "Each cause had its advocates, but they all wanted something from the alderman. He could do them good. They wouldn't want to hurt him."

"How about personality conflicts in the office?" Turner asked.

She shook her head. "Everybody was too busy. Working here was like the old days in the sixties. We all cared. Dedicated people who wanted to make the world a better place to be." She plucked a Kleenex from a box on the windowsill and dabbed at her eyes. "We accomplished a lot, and Gideon Giles was the reason. The causes will miss him, but I'll miss him more. He was a good, kind man. So much compassion."

"Can you tell us anything about his home life?" Turner asked.

"His wife has a career of her own. She's a commodities trader down on LaSalle Street. High-powered financial position. I've met her numerous times. Seemed to love Gideon. Was always supportive of his causes and his work, as he was of hers."

"Kids?" Fenwick asked.

"No children. They had their careers."

They asked about the movements of the people in the office between noon and one-thirty.

She drummed her fingers on the tabletop and thought. Finally she said, "On weekdays, it's pretty slow here. Weekends the place hums. Today we just had the regulars. Me, Audry the receptionist, and Hank, the legislative assistant."

"Where were they around noon?" Fenwick asked.

"We locked up the office and scattered. I had errands to run. I'm not sure where Audry and Hank went. It's Wednesday, so Hank probably went to pick up the weekly printing."

"Weekly printing?" Fenwick asked.

She pointed to the mounds of brochures around the room. "We do a large volume business with several local printers. Wednesday is the normal pickup day."

She gave them Audry and Hank's full names and addresses.

Fenwick rummaged through the campaign literature while Turner talked to two uniformed cops and Ashcroft about securing the office for the night. Turner finished and walked over to Fenwick. His partner held up two fistfuls of brochures. "Look at these," he said. "Got to be hundreds of them."

Turner glanced at them. "Bring one of each along," he said. "We can go over them later." He doubted if the printed ramblings would do anything but waste time.

They left the campaign office at seven, and returned to Area Ten headquarters. At their desks they pulled out blank forms: Case Report, Major Crime Worksheet, Daily Major Incident Log, Supplementary Report. They began the tedious process of documenting everything they'd done that day.

The district commander stopped by at nine-thirty. He asked them how it was going. They told him. The commander shook his head. "I've got to have results on this. Get those interviews done on the campaign people and the family first thing tomorrow. The pressure is more pervasive than anything I've ever seen. I've got calls from the superintendent, a number of aldermen, and every other two-bit politician in the city. That doesn't count the press. Individually they're ignorable, but collectively it's tougher to stand up to them. This case is tough. One of the biggest murders in years in this town." He sighed. "Do what you can, but don't stay here forever tonight. You've got lives to live."

Fenwick and Turner left at midnight, having put a decent-sized dent in the paperwork, but with a great deal left to do.

T H R E E

Turner took Harrison to Halsted and then up to Taylor, past the darkened University of Illinois at Chicago campus. He saw Mrs. Talucci through her kitchen window. She looked up, saw him, got up, walked to the window, and threw up the sash. The evening was pleasantly cool.

"You're up late," Paul said.

"Can't sleep," she said. "Old muscles start to ache." When she learned he hadn't had supper, she insisted he come in and have a bite. He sat at her modern butcher-block table. Mrs. Talucci handed him containers of food from the refrigerator. A trade paperback with the title *Applied Quantum Mechanics* lay open on the table.

Paul asked, "You going back for another degree?"

Casting about for something to do after her husband died, Mrs. Talucci had begun taking courses at the nearby University of Illinois campus. In the past twenty years she'd graduated from three different universities, accumulating one bachelor's and two master's degrees. The degree in philosophy had been from the University of Chicago.

She shoved the book aside. "I thought it might put me to sleep," she said. "I didn't understand much of the first chapter and that was just an introduction. I know enough math to count my change. That's just fine with me."

Fifteen minutes later Paul sipped steaming homemade vegetable soup and ate Italian sausage smothered in thick red tomato sauce, covered with Parmesan and mozzarella cheese, all between slabs of bread baked that afternoon by Mrs. Talucci.

She drank some decaffeinated coffee to keep him company. "You got the case with the alderman," she said.

He nodded.

"When you called and said you didn't know what time you'd be home, I guessed. Only one case on the news today that takes that kind of attention. They always give you the toughest ones, the political ones."

"It's a job," Paul said.

She patted his hand. "And you're the best, but the reward for the best shouldn't always be more work. They've got other cops at that station."

He said, "Did you know this guy, Giles?"

"Never had a class from him. Heard about him. Saw him on television. Didn't know him."

"Any University gossip?"

She thought a minute. "Not that I remember."

"How about Sorenson, the head of the department."

"That pompous jerk is a suspect?" Mrs. Tallucci asked.

Paul shrugged. "As much as anybody at the moment."

"He taught a seminar on Philosophical Positivism in Nineteenth-century British Novels. Worst course I ever had. We all knew more than he did. Couldn't define positivism. Couldn't cite passages in George Eliot. An absolute fool. I would have dropped the course, but I needed it for my degree."

Paul finished his dinner and walked home.

A cloudy Thursday morning, spring forgotten, a sharp wind blowing off Lake Michigan. Paul threw on a bulky knit sweater. His turn to cook breakfast.

Brian came in and plunked his baseball uniform, cap, and glove on the table.

"Not on the table." Paul's directive was almost as automatic as was Brian's retrieval of his gear and placing it on a chair. Paul wondered why his teenager couldn't make the connection of uniform not on table on the first try.

Jeff swung into the kitchen, took Brian's debris off the chair, and tossed it on the step stool. Jeff sat in the now vacant chair.

A few minutes later around a homemade waffle Brian said, "Coach thinks a few scouts from college teams and maybe even the major leagues will be around to watch us in a few weeks."

"You gonna be a star?" Jeff asked.

"I'm already a star," Brian said. "I want to be a pro."

"How does the coach know?" Paul asked.

"He says he's got contacts," Brian said.

Paul was proud of the athletic ability of his son, but he didn't want the teenager living in a fantasy world of professional possibilities. He knew Brian was good and would like his son to go as far as he could, but he wanted him to get a good education.

Jeff said, "I'm in the third round of the chess championship at school next week."

"How'd you get so good at chess?" Brian asked.

"Mrs. Talucci showed me a few tricks. Then I borrowed a computer chess game from a friend. I can get to level five out of nineteen."

"I'd like to see a game," Paul said.

"It's during school, Dad. If I get to the championship then it's after school."

"I'll come too," Brian said.

Paul assumed he'd be late because of the new case so before they left, he and his sons checked and rearranged schedules.

The cops in Area Ten spent roll call with the usual routine: important cases from the shifts before, directives from police headquarters at Eleventh and State, appointments for the day.

"Gideon Giles is top priority," Sergeant Poindexter said. "Any help Turner and Fenwick need, they get."

"I've got court at two this afternoon at Twenty-sixth and California," Turner said.

Poindexter frowned at him.

Turner said, "I don't go, I get written up. I ruin six months of work." If you failed to show up in court on a case you worked on, you could be in serious trouble. Being in court twice in one week wasn't at all unusual.

"You'll have to work even later," Poindexter informed him.

Turner nodded. He'd expected a long day.

Poindexter cornered Turner at the end of roll call. "The commander wants results. You and Fenwick have got to produce."

Yes, he and Fenwick always got the tough cases, but Turner barely had time to worry about the anomaly that those who worked the hardest got rewarded with more work and seldom more pay.

Randy Carruthers bustled up to Turner in the middle of the squad room. "Heard you guys were hip-deep in politics," the fresh-faced younger detective said.

Randy wore clothes whose tightness indicated recently gained weight. Frequently he carried at least one catalogue from a law school. He talked most often about taking law courses, so he could "get out of this hellhole and get a real job." Turner wished him all the luck in the world. He occasionally thought of secretly writing to every law school in the state for catalogues and giving them to Carruthers. On the other hand, as of yet, Paul had seen no evidence of law or any type of classes taken or passed. He ignored Carruthers and headed for his desk.

Carruthers peppered Fenwick with questions until Turner's partner growled at the young man, who then slunk away. Fenwick dumped his bulk at his desk, which abutted head-to-head with Turner's. They made their plans for the day.

First they needed to hunt for Frank Ricken, the campaign manager. The address they had, led them to a condo in Dearborn Village, just south of the Loop. Fenwick's racing progress left a wake of screeching tires and honking horns.

On the way Fenwick talked about his latest money-making scheme. He'd been reading the *Wall Street Journal* and had decided he could now make a million on the stock market. Buck always seemed to have one plan or another for making huge amounts of money very quickly. Madge would let him concoct elaborate scenarios for these castles in the air and then put her foot down.

After all these years, Turner listened with only half an ear, but at one point in their drive over, Turner made the mistake of saying, "Don't people with years of training sometimes lose a lot of money in the market?"

"I won't lose. I've got a system." The mercifully short drive gave Fenwick barely enough time to get into the basics of his plan.

Dearborn Park was an upscale area of condos and town homes anchored on the north end by the old Dearborn Station and Printer's Row section of the Loop. Old railroad right-of-ways bordered most of the land to the west and south.

They stood outside the door in the chill wind. Fenwick pounded on the bell, banged on the door, and shouted Ricken's name.

One curious neighbor stuck a head out.

Turner caught Fenwick's arm to forestall another assault on the door.

"We can come back later with a warrant," Turner said.

They walked two doors down to the neighbor who'd stuck her head out. They identified themselves, and she invited them in. A gargantuan brown ceramic ashtray and a huge poster of Chicago's skyline dominated the room they sat in. A woman in her early thirties, she said, "I can't talk long. I've got to get to my office."

Turner noted the briefcase next to the front door. He asked her to tell them as much as she could about Frank Ricken.

"Causes," she said. "Lots of causes. Ricken thought he could get free legal advice from my husband. Ricken would saunter over any time he felt like it and assume we'd drop everything to listen to him. Guy had a hell of a nerve."

"He bug the other neighbors?" Turner asked.

"He always wanted donations. Most everybody was used to him. He'd back off if you sounded at all put out. He'd come to summer cookouts. Hung around with some of the other committed types."

Turner took down their names.

Fenwick asked, "You think he'd kill somebody?"

She stared at him. "Did he kill somebody?"

Fenwick said, "Right now we just want to talk to him."

The woman had no idea where Ricken might be. Knew he worked for Alderman Giles. Turner thanked her for the information. They left.

They knocked on the doors of the neighbors on both sides, across from, and behind Ricken. Nobody home. Lot of young working people in the area. They'd have to come back.

As they crossed the street behind the condo complex, Fenwick nudged Turner's arm and pointed. "Look at the stupid shit coming out of the garbage. He fell into that stack of black plastic bags."

Turner looked at the man flailing at the mounds of trash he'd fallen into. Turner began to run toward the man. He shouted over his shoulder, "It's Ricken!"

Fenwick began to lumber after him. Ricken had also heard the shout. After a few more seconds of stumbling about, he got to his feet and dashed down the street.

They ran up State Street. Past the Pacific Garden Mission and Jones Commercial High School, where Ricken took a sharp left. Before he turned the corner, Turner glanced back. Fenwick was a block behind and rapidly falling further behind.

The chase continued down Harrison, two blocks west to Dearborn and back south again. The few pedestrians out on the streets at this time of the day glanced at him oddly, but didn't interfere. Turner kept Ricken in sight. He didn't have enough breath to shout for Ricken to stop, and only cops in the movies pulled out guns and had enough time to stop, aim, and shoot a fleeing suspect at a hundred paces. Shooting while running at top speed only made sense if you were shooting at a target the size of an elephant holding still. Plus Turner and the department frowned on shooting unarmed civilians in the back. Turner did try holding his radio to his mouth and calling in their situation, all while running full tilt.

Turner was in good shape, but Ricken was no slouch at speed. Turner saw him streak into Dearborn Station. Built in the heyday of the railroad barons in Chicago, the red brick station sat athwart Dearborn Street. The entire structure had recently been rehabilitated and now had a mini mall running down its center. The old clock tower on top of the building rose four stories above the pavement.

Turner paused inside the doorway, took a couple deep breaths, and called in his position and request for assistance.

Most of the shops were still closed at that hour, but bright lights gleamed halfway down the mall in a deli on the left. Turner hurried to the counter. A man with his hair pulled back in a ponytail was scrubbing the glass in the deli case.

"A man just run in here?" Turner asked.

The guy stared at him. Turner ripped out his ID, shoved it in the guy's face, and repeated his question.

"Nobody running. I think somebody walked in a few minutes ago."

"Where'd he go?"

The guy thought a second. Turner barely restrained his impatience. Finally the man pointed toward the stairs to the tower.

"You sure?" Turner asked.

"Sort of." The guy shrugged.

Turner paused at the bottom of the steps and gazed up. Fenwick ran in. "I stopped to call back." He gasped, drew ragged breaths, put one hand out to lean against a wall.

Turner explained what the witness had said. They agreed that Turner would explore the tower while Fenwick would stay at ground level in case Ricken slipped by him.

Turner drew his gun and proceeded cautiously up the steps. He paused at each landing, listened intently, then inched an eye around the corner to look. The second floor of the tower contained several businesses, all with darkened interiors. At the third landing he heard a floorboard creak. He couldn't tell if it was himself, the building being old, or the man he was pursuing. He listened for several heartbeats before rounding the corners, but each time he found nothing. As he ascended, he tried every door, but none of them gave way to his twisting of the knobs and pushing at the wood. He crept all the way to the top, checking every crevice and doorway. The last turn led him to a flight of steps that ended in a platform landing. Almost on hands and knees he eased his way from step to step. From what he could see before he began his climb, the room must be an observation deck. He sensed no one else's presence. His wider view of the room as he ascended the stairs confirmed the feeling. At the top step he made sure to check for any corners, doors, or hiding places before stepping into the room. Nothing. He looked out the windows. No way down except jumping. He saw Fenwick in the street below directing several uniformed cops.

Turner put his gun back under his coat and hurried down the stairs.

On the first floor he thought of bellowing a few chosen words at the guy in the deli, then forgot about it. Wouldn't do any good. He strode toward the entrance.

Fenwick was just opening the door, when a figure darted out of the shadows on Turner's left. Turner shouted. It was Ricken. The man ran straight toward Fenwick.

"Grab him!" Turner yelled.

Fenwick put up a hand as if he were halting traffic. Ricken plowed into him. Fenwick bellowed as he fell, grasping his wrist in pain and kicking out. Turner couldn't tell if this last was a reflex or deliberately planned. Whichever it was meant to be, it had the desired effect. Ricken got caught up in Fenwick's legs and fell to the ground.

Turner rushed over, whipped out a pair of handcuffs, and snapped them on a thrashing Ricken.

Fenwick held his wrist and mixed curses at Ricken with grumbling moans. Finally he bellowed, "If this is broken, you dumb shit, I will personally bust your face off!"

Ricken hunched his shoulders and tried to squirm away from the angry cop. Moments later the backup cops flooded into the station. Turner leaned against a pillar and watched them go through the dizzy dance of overresponse, telling each other everything was fine, staring at the prisoner, and talking to Fenwick and Turner.

Fenwick bent his hand back and forth. He said, "I think it's okay." He pointed a thumb at Ricken and said, "It'd feel a lot better if I could knock the shit out of that creep."

5 3

"I don't want to lose a bust because we're angry at him," Turner said reasonably. They taught cops to follow procedure. Sometimes it took years of going to court and realizing what judges threw out, to learn how to get a bust as close to perfect as possible. Some of the less-bright ones never learned. They might arrest a lot of people, but their conviction rates were horrible. Turner and Fenwick's record was excellent, but at times they had to help each other remember to stay calm, although Turner was called upon to perform this service more often than Fenwick. Buck's temper could be frightening.

"If you're okay, let's talk to him," Turner said.

Most of the tenants of the complex had come out to witness the police presence. The manager of the building told them they could use his office if they needed it. They sat Ricken in a wingback chair in a tiny room on the first floor. Turner stood at the window, the light behind his back, and Fenwick nursed his wrist while he sat on a diminutive couch next to the door.

"Why'd you run?" Turner asked.

"Am I accused of a crime?" Ricken asked.

"That attitude could get your face busted up and a trip to jail," Fenwick informed him.

"You wouldn't have caught me if I'd been able to find a back way out of this place," Ricken said.

"Taking off like that could still get you a couple years in prison," Fenwick said.

Ricken squirmed in his chair. "Do I have to have these cuffs on?" he asked.

"Be happy you aren't already in a holding cell," Fenwick said.

"I didn't kill Gideon Giles," Ricken said.

"What were you doing in the office yesterday?" Turner asked.

"I went to clean out my files."

"You were told to stay away," Turner said.

"I knew they'd all be at the press conference. I still had my key. I wanted to get my stuff without a hassle."

"Why'd you leave before we could question you? Why'd you run today?"

Ricken thought for several minutes before answering. He said, "I knew you'd find out I'd quarreled with Giles and the staff. I wanted to be ready for any questions. I didn't want to deal with the police. I was scared. I didn't think straight. I don't know. I'm not sure. I've never dealt with the police before."

"What'd you fight with Giles and the staff about?" Turner asked.

First Ricken gave them a history of his work with the alderman and the rest of the staff. Turner could see Fenwick's impatience, but they had Ricken talking. He wasn't demanding to see a lawyer. They hadn't read him his rights, because they hadn't charged him with a crime.

Ricken told them he started working for Giles in the alderman's first primary campaign many years ago. In college he'd majored in political science at the University of Illinois, Chicago. As an adult he'd wanted to be politically active. From the beginning, he and Giles hit it off. The staff for the first primary fight had been idealistic and dreamy-eyed. They'd lost, but four years later, the knowledge they'd gained paid off and they won. Giles hired Ricken as campaign manager just after the first unsuccessful primary fight.

"We always had a split in the office, between those of us who wanted to be realistic, get elected, be effective in the council, and those who wanted to put all the causes above everything else. The philosophically rigid and politically correct crowd usually had Gideon's ear, but the rest of us got through to him often enough to get him elected. Sometimes I thought Gideon actually believed in the causes, other times, who knows? I believed in him implicitly when I started. After ten years I began to have doubts. I expressed them. The true believers didn't like it. They capitalized on the ill feelings built up between the two factions to squeeze me further and further out of the mainstream. I thought I was the realist about office politics and internal bickering, but those do-gooders managed a vicious campaign."

"Anybody with specific grudges against Giles?" Turner asked.

"Not really. Most people liked him. He could be very charming."

Turner decided to go with a hunch. "You ran today because you've had trouble with the police before," Turner said.

Ricken stared at him, turned his face away to look out the window at the traffic on Dearborn Street.

"I like it that you're an ex-con," Fenwick said. "You may not want to tell us, but it will only take a couple seconds back at the station, but I'd especially like it if you tried to run again."

At the station they tried questioning him some more, but they got nowhere, and after a while Ricken started demanding to speak to a lawyer. Turner was for letting him go. "We don't really have anything on him," he said.

"What if he triest to run again? He did once," Fenwick said.

"Right now, let's let him go," Turner said. "We can have him followed. This case is big enough that we've got plenty of men assigned to it. I think it'll be interesting finding out where he goes."

Fenwick grumbled a bit more, but Turner convinced him. The minute after Ricken left, before he was out of sight, they had a tail on him.

They decided to try the neighbors of Laura and Gideon Giles. They lived in the middle of the block on Kenwood Avenue between Fifty-seventh and Fifty-eighth.

Fenwick parked the car in the driveway of the Giles's home. It was one of the few in the neighborhood with a driveway. They started with the house to the immediate north of the Giles's. A woman in a beige Christian Dior suit offered them tea, but knew little of the Giles. She said, "I don't get involved with University people." Turner thought she might have been referring as easily to cockroaches as to university professors.

To the south a woman in jeans and SAVE THE WHALES t-shirt welcomed them enthusiastically. She offered tea and gossip. About the woman in the Christian Dior outfit, she said, "Don't mind Sophie. She's had her nose in the clouds since her husband inherited half of some oil company. She's originally from some lower-class suburb. Got snubbed by University people long ago. Refuses to move, so she can be nasty to them. Nobody pays attention to her."

They sat in a room with polished wood floors and all solid teak furniture covered with an enormous variety of multicolored pillows. In contrast the walls were stark white and unadorned.

The woman's name was Dorinda Matthews. She brought out plates of cookies. Turner munched contentedly. They'd found the community gossip, generally one of the greatest sources for information.

Dorinda spoke with very little prodding. "I thought the police would be around. That Gideon Giles was a lunatic. Supporting all the fringe causes. We've got enough things in this neighborhood to fight for without worrying about obscure animals in the Yukon. Tenants rights, the homeless in the less well-off parts of the ward. Giles would be off after international politics. I mean we all care about human rights everywhere, but it starts at home. Don't you think?"

Turner let her ramble for several minutes then asked, "How did Mr. and Mrs. Giles strike you as a couple?"

"On the scale of one to ten of happily married, ten being wedded bliss, I'd have to give them a nine."

"No fights," Turner asked.

"Not while I was around and I'm here fairly often. I like to know my neighbors, and Laura and Gideon weren't too friendly. At first I thought it was because they had something to hide. Brought her an apple pie the first day. You'd of thought I was offering raw worms. I let them be. Only thing to mention was occasional late parties. Fund-raisers for some cause. You'd think they'd have invited the neighbors, but they didn't. No children, but this isn't the best kid neighborhood in the city."

In essence her information was that the Giles were a loving and devoted couple who as far as Dorinda knew rarely had fights.

Turner asked if the Giles's got along with the rest of the neighbors.

Dorinda said, "I think it was mostly like with me, not too close. They had their causes. This isn't a close-knit neighborhood, although a couple years ago they had a problem with Bruno Phelps, who lives across the alley from them."

"What was that about?" Turner asked.

"Trash cans. Somebody stole Bruno's. Never did find them. Accused Giles for some reason. Then when Giles became alderman, Bruno took every chance he got to say what a crook Giles was."

Next they tried the houses across the street. They got the same story about the Giles's aloofness from these neighbors but little more.

Bruno Phelps turned out to be an enormous man in his late seventies. He answered their knock and invited them in. Bruno spared little time explaining his dispute with Giles.

"I'm sure he had something to do with taking the trash cans. They'd just moved into the neighborhood. Snooty as all hell. Tried to get them in the neighborhood watch program. Wouldn't give a minute's time. Not interested in helping the guy next door. Don't like those kind of people."

Bruno had been on his fourth set of new trash cans, which he'd had to buy himself, when they were stolen again. "Giles didn't even care. Practically slammed his door in my face. Told me to get a life. I'm sure he had something to do with it."

Bruno spent fifteen more minutes adding illogic to silliness about the trash cans. Obviously the incident had been one of the seminal experiences of his retired life. He'd been a low-level administrator at the University for forty-two years before he retired ten years ago. He knew nothing of its current politics.

"Crazy old guy," Fenwick said as they left.

Turner looked at his list of people left to interview and sighed. "It's going to take forever," he said. "I wish that secretary Gwendolen was back in town." They'd found out yesterday that the secretary was on a European tour and wouldn't be back for several days. Turner wondered if the killer knew that and somehow took advantage of it.

They drove back to Area Ten headquarters. Turner had to be in court and Fenwick agreed to make some background phone calls and computer checks on the people they'd talked to. Turner thumbed through his messages. A number to call that he didn't recognize and a message with it that said "urgent." He tried the number and got a busy signal. At Twenty-sixth and California, he listened to the testimony of the medical examiner. The case involved a drive-by shooting witnessed by eleven people, five of whom had the presence of mind to write down the license number of the car that the shots burst from. The shooters had the ill luck or stupidity to drive around in the car for the next few hours. Turner and Fenwick had caught up with them at State and Congress Parkway when the beat cop reported the car double-parked outside the Burger King. The case was simple enough, but he had to testify.

During a break in the court proceedings he called Fenwick, but other than the delivery of all the papers from Giles's office nothing new had happened. Fenwick had three cops checking through the papers. He didn't hold out much hope for finding anything useful in them.

Turner tried the urgent message number again. He was almost ready to hang up, but on the seventh ring, an out-of-

59

breath person answered. Turner didn't recognize the voice on the other end of the phone. He identified himself.

"This is Clark Burke. I've got to see you." The university student sounded out of breath and worried.

After being sure the kid wasn't in immediate danger, Turner agreed to meet him at Ann Sather's Restaurant in Hyde Park, near the University. Turner testified for half an hour, called into the station, and drove to meet Burke.

He parked across the street from the restaurant on Fifty-seventh street and got out of the car. He saw Burke standing outside the front door of the restaurant. The kid wore a black leather jacket, faded jeans at least a size too small, and white running shoes. Pale spring sunlight peaked through gray clouds and glinted off the gold rims of Burke's glasses. Burke caught sight of the cop, gave Turner a beatific smile, quickly replaced by a nervous frown.

They sat in a booth next to the windows on the east side of the restaurant. Burke took off his black leather jacket to reveal a skintight t-shirt that showed off a slender, muscular frame.

I'm being seduced, Turner guessed. The first thought that crossed his mind was a cop's suspicious why, the second a tingle of flattery, and the last the memory that he had a son only a couple years younger than Burke.

Turner ordered coffee and a cinnamon roll, Burke a vegetable platter.

"You sounded pretty worried on the phone," Turner said.

"I was out of breath because I was talking to some guys in a room down the hall, and I had to run to catch the phone. I'm afraid to go to my room."

Turner raised an eyebrow. Burke's gray eyes followed the older man's continuously, maybe looking for approval, Turner thought, maybe reassurance.

Burke explained, "I got back to my room from class at noon. Somebody trashed the place."

"Did you call security?"

60

Burke shook his head. "I found this on the floor." He held out a three-by-five card.

Turner held it by the edges. The note threatened Burke by name with bodily harm, giving details of the pain that would be inflicted. Burke stared out the window. Turner glanced back at the note. The writer accused Burke of being a faggot and said he'd get the same treatment as Gideon Giles, saying that all left-wing intellectuals, faggots, feminists, and liberals had better beware.

Turner layed the note carefully on a napkin. All fingerprints of value had probably been long since destroyed, but he'd have it checked anyway.

Burke sat erect with his arms resting on the table. "I'm scared," he said. "I thought it would be better, coming to the city and being gay. That I'd left all that prejudice shit back in Chatsworth, Iowa."

"The University's had some trouble in the past few years with attacks against gays," Turner said. "This could simply be part of that."

Burke pointed to the card. "It mentions the murder."

"It could be part of that, or it could be a nut case trying to frighten people." Turner sighed. "Who has access to the dorm rooms?"

"We've got sort of security. Somebody down at a front desk. You can't get upstairs unless they know you or you've got some identification."

"So somebody living at the dorm did this?"

"Probably, but it's not that hard to get in without being noticed. Not if you're determined."

Their food arrived. Turner sipped at the coffee, Burke left his vegetables untouched. "They trashed my room. They busted my computer." Burke had tears in his eyes. "My parents spent a lot of money getting me one. They had to do without a lot, but they wanted me to have the best."

"I'm sorry about your computer. I'll have a look at your

room. We'll also call university security. Did you have a room-mate?"

"He dropped out last month."

"Any problems with him?"

"We were friends. He just couldn't hack the work." Burke picked at his food for several minutes. Turner ate some of his roll and waited for the kid to talk.

Finally Burke said, "I'm afraid to stay at the dorm."

"Don't you have a friend you could stay with, or I'm sure the university would put you up somewhere else."

Burke's deep voice became very soft. "I'm not sure. I guess I could ask around." This didn't at all sound like what he had in mind. Turner didn't pursue the topic. Silence fell between them, and Turner let it build.

"One thing," Burke said as the waitress brought the check. Turner nodded.

"I saw a picture of Mrs. Giles in the paper today. I'd never met her before. She never came around the office. I'm sure it was her I saw in the quadrangle the day before with Mr. Giles. I had an extra long lunch that day too. I saw the two of them in front of Swift Hall."

"Could you hear what they said?"

"No."

"Could she have been up to the office to meet him?" Turner asked.

"Maybe. He was still there when I left for lunch. You think that she was there the day before is important?"

"I don't know," Paul said. "We have no proof she went upstairs. We don't know if or where they had lunch. The office is open during noontime. Anyone could have stopped in, planted the poison, and left."

They walked to the dorm. Their bodies bumped inciden-tally as they strolled along. Turner couldn't tell if these touches were accidents or deliberate or had any meaning at all. He asked the woman at the front desk in the dorm to call security.

6 2

Burke's room was the last one on the right on the fifth floor.

In the room the words FAGGOTS DIE glared in bright yellow from the wall to the left of the door. Strewn across the top bunk were shirts, socks, jockey shorts, and handkerchiefs. Two drawers from the dresser stood at angles leaning against the walls. Ripped and torn remnants from the bottom bunk's mattress and pillow covered much of the floor. The closet door dangled from one hinge. The rest of the can of yellow paint had been dumped on the heap of clothes and twisted hangers. On the desk the smashed computer screen gaped helplessly at them.

"Must have made a lot of noise when this happened," Turner said.

"I asked the guys. Nobody was home. Do you think who-ever did it knew that?"

"Probably," Turner said.

Burke had tears in his eyes. "I didn't think hate like this existed."

Several of the other dorm students murmured in the door-way. Turner asked them a few questions but as Burke had said, none had been around. The students reassured Burke of their concern and support, then left. Turner shut the door, seated himself on the corner of the desk. Burke stood at the window looking out.

"Who on campus knows you're gay?" the cop asked.

"My friends."

"Gay or straight or both?"

"I only know a few gay people. I joined the gay organization on campus for a while, but with work and studying I just didn't have the time. I guess most of the guys on the floor knew. Nobody really cared. I thought."

"Any trouble before this?" Turner asked.

"No. I'd heard about the trouble you mentioned, but I never thought it would happen to me."

"I'm sorry it did," Turner said.

Nothing in the room was missing, as far as Burke could tell. "I saw the mess and called you. I only touched the phone." Burke assured him he hadn't handled anything else since he'd discovered the destruction.

"Let's get you a place to stay. Meanwhile I'll have evidence techs go over the room. Maybe they can find something useful."

Burke hesitated. He caught Turner's eyes, then quickly dropped his own and looked at the floor. He cleared his throat once or twice, reached to rearrange a stack of textbooks. Turner caught the hand and said, "It's best not to disturb anything." Burke didn't flinch at the touch. Turner didn't let the closeness linger.

They talked with campus security and the housing administrator. They found Burke temporary quarters and promised something more permanent by the next day. Turner reassured Burke, then left.

He drove to Area Ten headquarters. Fenwick greeted him with, "Where the hell have you been?"

Turner told him about the destruction of Burke's room.

Fenwick asked, "Connected with the murder?"

"I don't know. Why would the killer bother? We've got no connection of any significance between Giles and Burke. Nobody's questioned Giles's credentials as a certifiable straight man. I don't see a gay connection here."

"Odd coincidence," Fenwick said.

"Not if a nut case heard about Burke's connection to the murder and decided to be cruel at this time. Who knows? He also told me he saw Mrs. Giles the day before, talking to her husband in the quadrangle during the noon hour."

"Why didn't he mention it before?" Fenwick asked.

"Said he didn't know her. Saw a picture in the paper today and put the two together."

"Or he could have been lying yesterday," Fenwick said.

"Why lie?" Turner asked.

Fenwick shrugged. "I guess we have to interview Mrs. Giles again."

Turner found the Giles's phone number and called. No answer. "Probably with a friend," Turner said. He remembered the woman who brought Mrs. Giles to the office the day before. He got Lilac Ostergard's number from his notes and called. No answer there either. He'd try again later.

"What'd you find out on background?" Turner asked.

Fenwick tossed over a computer printout. "You were right. Our buddy Ricken does have a criminal record. I've got a call out to pick Ricken up again," Fenwick said.

Turner glanced at the printout. "An assault case? Nearly fifteen years old? For this you're having him picked up?"

"He attacked a cop," Fenwick said.

"At a campus demonstration when he was still in his teens. How do you connect that with murder now?"

"Attacking a cop. He could be capable of violence."

"You're just pissed because he roughed you up a little bit." Fenwick growled.

Turner stifled a sigh. "I guess it won't hurt to talk to him. What did you get on the university people?"

"Preliminary check on them showed all clean records. Same for the campaign people. I had time to get to the most important ones."

"We have the interviews of all the other people in the building?" Turner asked. He'd assigned several uniforms to questioning anyone who had been in the English department offices or in the building the day before.

Fenwick handed him a sheaf of papers.

"They find anything?" Turner asked.

"Nobody remembers any strangers, but there's people in and out of that building all the time. There's a small cafeteria in the basement, so all kinds of people use it."

Turner looked at the list of contacted people. Fenwick had divided them up into a columns, one for people from the ward organization and campaign staffs, the other for the university community.

Turner heard a thump and then Fenwick swearing. He glanced across the double desk. No Fenwick. He looked on the side. Fenwick was on his hands and knees, picking up the hundreds of brochures he'd taken from the campaign head-quarters. He got up puffing and red-faced. "I've been going through these," he said, as he restacked them on his desk. One slipped off the tallest pile, but he managed to grab it before it fell to the floor. "There's something odd about these," he said.

"How so?" Turner asked.

"I don't know. I spent a long time going over them while you where gone. Something I can't figure out, I don't know what it is."

Turner was willing to spend a great deal of time checking into any insight or hunch Fenwick might have. They'd been partners long enough to respect each other's cop intuition.

"I just can't put my finger on it," Fenwick said. He shrugged.

"Maybe you'll think of it later," Turner said. He switched topics. "We get anything from the medical examiner or from the crime lab?" Turner asked.

"Not yet," Fenwick said.

Turner reached for the phone. He glanced at the clock on the wall. After five. People might be gone for the day. He waded through several layers of bureaucrats before he got to Sam Franklin.

"Poison," Sam told him. "Nicotine. In the opened unla-beled juice jar."

"Nicotine," Turner said. "I didn't know you could do that."

"Sure," Sam said. "I know of one case where a woman took the residue of several cigarette butts, put them in a jug of water, strained it, and put the poisoned water where the victim would drink it, and bingo. One dead body. Doesn't take much."

"I guess not. He wouldn't notice the taste?" Turner asked.

"Real doubtful," Franklin said. "What he concocted you'd have to gulp down practically holding your nose."

Turner thanked him. When he hung up, Fenwick said, "I've got the full-time political people meeting us at his campaign headquarters."

Turner checked his watch. Already five-thirty and nowhere near done for the day. He called home and checked with Brian. He also talked with Ben Vargas briefly. They had no plans for the night, but Turner wanted to hear his voice.

At the campaign headquarters, twenty people milled around the front room. Fenwick entered, called for silence, and told them they'd be interviewed one by one.

Turner had checked the list of political people with Fenwick before they left Area Ten. He assigned two more uniformed cops to interview the part-time volunteers. He'd rather have interviewed all of them himself. You never knew when a right question would trigger a unique response that might yield a clue or a suspect. No way he'd have enough time to get to all of them.

By eight they had two left to talk to. They'd been using the inner office. Turner rubbed his hand across his eyes then asked, "Who's next?"

Fenwick said, "I saved the biggest for last. The media consultant and a brother-in-law."

Turner said, "So far tonight we've found out he was an absolute saint, and every single person we talked to had an alibi. I was hoping to get a little more from that Audrey and Hank who were working here yesterday. Their alibis seem good." Turner thought of all the forms they'd have to fill out for everybody they'd interviewed in the past few hours. He groaned.

"You okay?" Fenwick asked.

"Yeah. Let's get it over with and get out of here."

Fenwick ushered in a tall, white-haired man in an impeccably tailored charcoal suit. If he was annoyed at being made to wait for hours, he didn't show it.

"Jack Stimpson," Fenwick announced.

He'd been the media consultant for every one of Giles's tries for office.

Stimpson spoke in pleasant but firm tones. He explained that Giles was congenitally unable to lose his temper. That the former alderman could listen to every side of an issue and see reason on everyone's part.

"He didn't look like that at city council meetings I saw on TV," Fenwick said.

"All an act for the media. Giles was always a master at manipulating them. He could get more done, more attention for a cause with a simple press conference than many groups who worked for years."

"Did they resent him for usurping their turf?" Turner asked.

"Far from it. They appreciated his support. Attention from Gideon could skyrocket an organization's fund-raising ability and effectiveness."

"His bills never got passed in the city council," Turner pointed out.

"But the causes were put forward. Attention was paid. That's why he's got the largest political staff in the city. He received lots of money from the causes. He could afford all this hired help."

Turner asked about the Giles's married life.

"I was his best friend. My wife and I spent many pleasant hours with them. They were very happy."

"How about Frank Ricken?" Turner asked.

"A loser, but he had presence. He could fool the media with the best of them, but a whiner. Ricken may have been Gideon's first volunteer. Much of the success with the campaigns came about because of him. He was a master at milking a photo opportunity. The past few months he became enamored with several pet causes. Wanted more attention for them. Began neglecting his job."

"Do you know anything about Ricken's private life?" Turner asked.

"Whenever an attractive young woman volunteered for the organization, you could see Ricken zeroing in on her. He didn't have a great deal of charm. My impression is that he failed more often than not."

Turner asked about Giles's relationship with his wife.

"He often talked about how happy he was. He mentioned his good relations with his wife, not in a vulgar way, but I could tell he was happy."

"Any disagreements with anybody else?" Turner asked.

"No. We all worked well together," Stimpson said.

"We were told the various groups fought for his attention," Turner said.

"Only because people believed, not because people were angry with each other or willing to do murder," Stimpson said.

Last was the brother-in-law, Alex Hill. He was somber and soft-spoken. He shook hands with the two police officers gravely. He looked to be about five years younger than his sister Laura.

"I'm willing to do anything I can to help you find the killer," he announced. He sat down, crossed his right ankle onto his left knee, and favored them with a solemn look.

They asked about his duties with the campaign. He'd been a speech writer and, before that, worked for a suburban newspaper writing articles mostly on meetings of small local groups. "I was the tea-and-crumpets reporter. If any kind of group got together, we went out and took their pictures. People love to see their names in the paper."

They asked him about the campaign and possible enemies. He didn't know of any. He'd simply come to the office and write speeches appropriate for whichever occasion and group. The detectives didn't find him helpful and let him go.

It was nine. He'd tried calling Laura Giles several times during the interviewing and gotten no answer. He tried again with the same result. As they climbed into the car, Turner said, "We've got time to get to the former ward committeeman's house. We've gotten nowhere so far today. I want to give him a try."

Turner looked up the address on his master list. Five minutes later they pulled up in front of the home of the former Fifth Ward committeeman on Woodlawn Avenue just north of Fifty-fifth Street. The house covered three normal-sized lots and had driveways on both sides.

Fenwick whistled. "Old Mike McGee sure did okay for himself."

"I didn't know you cared about politics," Turner said.

"Usually I couldn't give a shit what these politicians do," Fenwick said, "but everybody knew Mike McGee. I grew up on the southwest side hearing stories about the fights he won for the little guy."

Turner sighed. "We never heard much about him on the near west side." Chicago neighborhoods tended to be tremendously insular. Denizens of ethnic or racial enclaves not your own were at best totally ignored, at worst outright enemies.

McGee as committeeman would be less well known than the alderman, but possibly more powerful. The alderman was simply a legislative representative with set duties. The committee man was an unpaid party representative who controlled patronage. This meant an army of precinct workers whose civil service–exempt jobs depended on how well they performed on election days. No law gave the committeeman such power over jobs, but custom and the Democratic party did. Being both alderman and committeeman was the ultimate combination.

As they walked up to the front porch they saw a lamp shining in the front room. The light gleamed off rows of books in floor-to-ceiling bookcases.

Fenwick punched the doorbell. Turner heard soft distant chimes. A young woman answered the door and looked at them curiously. They showed her their identification. In the light spilling from the interior, she examined each star carefully. Finally satisfied, she let them into a dimly lit front hall.

Turner thought she looked to be about thirty, slender and blond, with tortoiseshell glasses and a grave smile. He explained why they'd come.

She spoke softly. "I take care of my grandfather. He's not well, and he is usually asleep in his chair by this time. I'll see if I can wake him." She walked down the hallway, opened a door, light streamed out for a moment. Darkness returned as she moved into the room and shut the door.

"Hot stuff," Fenwick whispered.

"Attractive, but not my type," Turner whispered back. He examined his surroundings. They were in a foyer with a coat and hat rack. Dark wood paneling ran halfway up to the ceiling. Light yellow wallpaper with a repeating dark-green ivy pattern covered the top half of the entry-room walls. The door reopened. The woman reappeared. You didn't hear her footfalls on the thick dark-green carpet.

She said, "He'll see you for a while. He gets tired very easily."

She ushered them into the room she'd returned from.

"Bring them here, Molly." The old voiced rasped and crackled. They entered the room with the bookcases they'd seen lit from outside.

Mike McGee wore a gray suit, white shirt, and green tie, all neatly pulled together as if he might leave in a few moments for a day at the office, but he also had a shawl around his shoulders and another around his knees, as he sat in an overstuffed chair with his feet flat on the floor.

A ten-inch television screen near the man's elbow showed a press conference. Mike McGee made a shushing motion and hunched a little closer to the picture. Turner listened and watched. On the screen a gaggle of alderman stood in front of a bank of microphones. Each of the city's representatives in turn made angry denunciations of the mayor and the police while demanding bodyguards and twenty-four-hour protection for themselves. Turner swallowed his annoyance. Each theatrical display like that only added pressure to the cops, but never helped solve a case. McGee waited until the segment was over, then shut off the television and leaned back.

Molly McGee stood next to her grandfather, one hand on the back of the chair, the other resting on her hip, not defiant but definitely protective.

"Tell me when you want them to leave, Grandfather," she said.

He smiled up at her, touched her hand gently. "Will you bring us some tea, Molly? These gentlemen are here to discuss murder." She looked doubtful but after a moment complied with the old man's wishes.

Turner gazed at Mike McGee's face. He knew he was gazing

at a Chicago institution. McGee had begun as committeeman of the Fifth Ward just after Anton Cermak got elected mayor. He'd survived the wars and revolutions in the Cook County Democratic party until Gideon Giles came along. Finally retired, a grand old man of the party, revered in a few corners, but no longer feared, certainly not consulted.

Turner had never seen so many freckles on a human countenance. Over and around the sunken flesh and mottled crevices a blizzard of freckles shone brightly. His clothes seemed a little large on him and Turner guessed McGee might have been somewhat stout at one time. Now he seemed to be shrunken with the years.

"I expected you here before this," McGee said. The old voice might crack with age, but Turner heard steel and firmness underneath. This was a man used to giving orders and being obeyed.

"We were wondering if you could give us any information that might help," Turner said.

"I know everybody's dirty little secrets," McGee said. "I know everything."

McGee insisted that they pull up green leather armchairs to form a circle around a marble-topped coffee table, inlaid in its center with a map of Ireland. Molly McGee laid out a tea service, a silver pot, small sandwiches, cookies that looked home-baked, dark-green mugs, all on a mirror-surfaced tray.

Turner sipped from his cup of tea and placed it on a cocktail table with a dark-green lace doily. He glanced at Fenwick. He noted his partner trying to conceal his normal cynicism.

Molly resumed her place standing by her grandfather's side.

"Now boys," he began. The remnants of the Irish brogue made the soft voice soothing and melodious. "Now boys," McGee reiterated, "I've got stories I could tell you that would turn the hair on your head gray. I know everything about the real politics of this city." He chuckled softly.

"Sir," Fenwick said, "we hoped you could tell us something about Gideon Giles."

"A lowlife. A bum. Not worth the spit to shine a beggar's shoes."

"He ousted you as committeeman," Turner said.

"No he didn't. No he didn't. Not by a long shot."

"Grandfather," Molly soothed, patting his shoulder gently.

He brushed off her hand. As he attempted to stand, the shawl on his knees slipped to the floor. He fell back in frustration a moment later, a pang of agony shooting across his face, but he wouldn't accept Molly's arm as help. He shook his fist at Turner. "That bastard wasn't worthy to clean my mother's toilets."

"You mean he didn't have the right to run against you," Fenwick said.

Mike McGee glared at Fenwick. "He had every right. He just never should have won."

Fenwick said, "The liberals ran you out of office even after years of running a tight ship."

"I'm one of the liberals, you young fool." McGee shook a withered and trembling finger at Fenwick. "This is a good ward. Tough politics. Should have had a black alderman years ago, but I gave everybody in this ward good service, black-white, rich-poor, everybody. That idiot Giles thought I was too old. I didn't take him seriously. A professor from the university. What did he know about politics? Bastard stole the election."

Again McGee tried to rise and this time, despite the pain, managed it. He rested a hand on the back of an armchair.

Molly said, "Grandfather," and reached to help him. He waved her away.

The woman said to the police, "Surely you don't believe my grandfather walked all the way to the university, up numerous flights of stairs, and murdered this man. People would recognize him. Certainly someone would have reported seeing him."

"We just want information," Turner said.

"It's all right, Molly. Let them ask."

"I don't understand about the election," Turner said. "Were your referring to when he became committeeman or alderman?"

"Both." The old man sighed. "I didn't take him seriously when he ran for alderman in the first primary. He lost. Four years later he tried again. I should have paid more attention. He won that election. I thought I was ready for him two years ago, but he managed to steal the ward from under me."

"How did he do that?" Turner asked.

The old man shut his eyes for several minutes. When he opened them he said, "Gideon Giles stopped by here around twelve-thirty the day he was murdered," McGee said.

Molly gasped and put her hand to her lips. McGee glared at her. His long gray eyebrows twitched, then drew together.

"Molly didn't know," McGee said. "I let him in."

Turner wondered about the change in topic, and he doubted strongly that McGee had let his enemy in, but he could talk to Molly about that later.

"What did he want?" Turner asked.

"Help in his next election."

"Surely he couldn't expect that from a man he defeated."

"Politics. Everybody wants something. Claimed he was afraid he might lose the next election."

"I thought he was real popular," Fenwick said.

"He was worried about something, but he wouldn't tell me what. Wanted my help though. I told him it would cost him."

"What was your price?" Turner asked.

"Favors. That's what politics in Chicago runs on. You do something for me, I do something for you. I wanted favors, and the politically pure Gideon Giles wouldn't deal."

"That's his reputation," Turner said. "Why would he change now?"

McGee chuckled. "My boy, you are refreshing," McGee said. "You don't know much about human nature, do you?"

Turner gave him a puzzled look but kept silent. If the man wanted to talk, he'd let him.

McGee took his time rearranging himself in his chair, pulling his shawls more tightly around himself, patting the wrinkles out of his pants and suit jacket with elaborate care.

McGee began, "He sold his soul to someone," then lowered his voice to continue, "and that bothered the saintly Mr. Giles, and he wanted out of the deal he made with the devil. But whoever the devil's representative was this time wasn't going to let him out of the contract. He sold his soul, and he came crawling to me for help and forgiveness."

The old man again shut his eyes for a few minutes. He pulled in several deep breaths. Turner felt the dimly lit old room gather oppressively close around him. He glanced at Fenwick. His partner tried concealing an irritated glare. Turner looked at Molly now standing several feet from her grandfather. She had her arms folded across her chest.

"Did he say who he was afraid of or what deal he wanted to get out of?" Turner asked.

"No. I threw him out." McGee laughed. "You see, young man, I wanted revenge. I believe in revenge. I watched that young man sweat and squirm, because his conscience was torturing him. I didn't kill him. I wanted him to live a long and miserable life, knowing he sold out, just like all the people he's made a life out of criticizing. I hope he's rotting in hell."

"We were told you might have been siphoning off campaign funds for personal use," Turner said. "That Giles threatened you with it, and that's when he ran against you."

"Lies," the old man said. "Silly rumors, repeated by people who don't know anything about politics. You can look up every financial record or statement of mine. I never took a thing."

They left a few minutes later without learning anything further. It was late and Turner simply wanted to get home.

In the car their radio crackled to life. Turner responded. The nasal voice of the dispatcher informed them that they were wanted at Ricken's house.

"What's up?" Turner asked.

"Don't know. I'm supposed to tell you to get over there."

They returned to the Dearborn Park condominium complex. Outside they saw a blue-and-white cop car, an unmarked Plymouth, and the white van with CHICAGO CRIME LAB printed on the side.

In the front room of the condo a row of windows filled with the velvet night of early spring faced east. Lining one wall was motion modular furniture in natural textures with blue, beige, and mauve accent pillows. A large-screen television filled another wall. A painting of a pale yellow flower surrounded by gauzy white background hung over on the third wall. The fourth end led into a kitchen. A cereal bowl with a remnant of milk in the bottom and a glass with a residue of orange juice rested in the sink. A young cop near the refrigerator pointed toward a hallway.

Wading through the bustle of the working cops from the crime lab, Turner made his way into a bedroom. There he found Joe Roosevelt and Judy Wilson, two other detectives from Area Ten. A smashed mirror leaned at a forty-five degree angle against one wall. Two halves of a trophy lay on the floor. Shards of glass covered large areas of the floor and bed.

"What happened?" Turner asked.

Wilson pointed to a spot on the floor on the opposite side of the room. Turner craned his neck around a beefy crime-lab tech. In the middle of a multihued throw rug was a dark ugly stain larger around than a basketball.

"Where's Ricken?" Turner asked.

"Tail lost him around seven," Wilson said. "He went back to district headquarters. Should have come here. Neighbors called half an hour ago. Said they heard a violent quarrel, lots of smashing glass. We got the call and hurried over. Knew he was the guy you were looking for. Door was standing open when we got here. Nobody around. You'll see faint traces of blood between here and the door."

"We already have people checking the hospitals to see if he showed up for treatment," Roosevelt said.

While evidence technicians swarmed around them, Turner gave Roosevelt and Wilson the highlights of what they'd found out that day.

Roosevelt and Wilson had been detectives since the year one. Joe Roosevelt, red-nosed, with short, brush-cut gray hair and bad teeth, and Judy Wilson, an African-American woman with a pleasant smile, had a well-deserved reputation as one of the most successful pairs of detectives on the force.

"This has got to be connected," Wilson said.

Turner nodded. "But I don't know how."

"I hate coincidences," Roosevelt said. "Too close together. Happening so soon after Giles gets it, got to mean something."

"Anything preliminary on the scene here?" Turner asked.

"No sign of a forced entry," Roosevelt said. "Must of known the attacker or he had confidence enough to let him in. We don't know if anything is missing. Lots to find out."

The four nodded agreement. They worked out a method of sharing information and dividing up people to interview. Since Fenwick and Turner had started on the political people, they would continue with them. Wilson and Roosevelt would concentrate on Ricken's family, friends, and neighbors not connected to Gideon Giles and politics.

At the station, Turner turned in his radio at the equipment room and walked toward his desk. Sergeant Poindexter cornered him near the coffee machine. "Got to get something on this case. Can't have an alderman getting shot and now his campaign manager missing under suspicious circumstances."

Turner wanted to tell him to give it a rest, but the guy was his superior officer. Turner gave a brief rundown of their activities.

"We need results," Poindexter said.

Turner managed to escape from Poindexter after fifteen minutes. He glanced at his watch. Almost midnight. He felt frustrated investigating all the politics of the murder. He wanted information, and he knew where he could probably get it. At his desk he dialed Ian Hume.

He knew Ian would be awake at this hour. His friend seldom retired before two or three in the morning.

Ian Hume was the star reporter for the city's gay newspaper, the *Gay Tribune*. Three years ago he'd won the Pulitzer prize for investigative journalism for his exposé of the medical establishment's price-fixing for AIDS drugs.

Turner and Hume had gone through the police academy together and had been assigned the same district as beat cops. They'd come to respect and like each other. Ian had gotten fed up with the bureaucracy, and also decided to come out sexually. He'd quit the department to work full-time as a reporter. They had been lovers for a brief time after Turner's wife died. Now they were occasionally of some help to each other on cases.

Ian answered by saying, "I'm on my way out the door. If this isn't sexy and interested, hang up."

Turner explained what he needed.

Ian said, "I don't have the kind of connections that would give me real dirt on City Hall types."

"How about Mary Ann Eliot?" Turner asked.

Mary Ann Eliot, born to southwest side working-class Irish parents, now represented the upscale, lakefront Forty-third ward. The first openly lesbian candidate elected to the city council, she'd worked her way up through the regular Democratic organization. Spent years ringing doorbells, getting out the vote, and carrying her precinct. She scorned the trendy liberal set and really believed in the concept that good government is good politics. Her aplomb and expertise in dealing with hostile elements at campaign stops was legendary. The last fundamentalist preacher who attended one of her rallies left with welts on his ego and holes in his spirituality. Turner and Ian had worked as volunteers in her campaign. Turner had met her once, but didn't think she'd remember him.

"She might be able to tell us inside political information," Turner said. "I don't know of any other source in the city. She probably won't remember me, but you know her. I'd like to talk with her."

Ian agreed to set up the meeting, even going so far as to promise to get up early the next morning to make the calls.

It was past one when Turner walked in his front door.

Brian lay with his arms crossed, head resting on them, atop his calculus book. The kitchen radio was turned to a classical music station. Brian usually listened to incomprehensible rock music while he did his homework, but calculus drove him nuts, and one evening in a vain attempt to find a soothing break from wrestling with higher math, while scanning through the FM band, he discovered a Brahms symphony. Brian refused to admit he liked the music, just said he found it restful at these difficult times.

Paul shook him gently. "You need to get to bed."

"What time is it?" Brian rubbed his fist against his eyes.

"Late," Paul said. Brian stumbled up the stairs. Paul looked in on Jeff. Tired as he was, he sat on the edge of his younger son's bed and watched him sleep before hugging him gently and going up to his own room.

Next morning Turner strode in seconds before roll call started. After the morning folderol with the watch commander and duty sergeant, the Area Ten commander called Turner, Fenwick, Randy Carruthers, and Harold Rodriguez into his office.

The commander said, "It's been three days. I have no results to show anybody. Normally I can handle the pressure, but this is the worst I've ever seen. I've got someone here from Eleventh and State just to answer calls from the media. I need to know what's going on." The lack of his usual mild and calm demeanor confirmed to Turner that the commander must be under enormous pressure.

Turner filled the group in on what they'd done since the murder. He finished, "We've got too many suspects."

Carruthers said, "Giles knew a zillion people. We've got even more to grill today." Carruthers still used words like "grill." Turner often thought he must have learned how to be a cop from watching old gangster movies.

Turner managed to convince the commander that Carruthers should interview all the major political contributors and heads of all the liberal reform operations. These had to be covered on the unlikely chance one of them knew something.

Turner got Laura Giles on the phone the first time he called. She said she'd been at a friend's the night before. Turner asked her about meeting Gideon Giles the day before for lunch. She sounded as if she were holding back tears as she said, "It was the last time we had lunch together. We did it once in a while." No, she hadn't gone up to the English office. They'd run over to the Medici restaurant in Harper Court. Turner knew that so far the beat cops doing the secondary interviews of all the people who worked in the building hadn't found anyone who saw Mrs. Giles in the English department anytime Monday or Tuesday until after the murder.

Fenwick drove at his usual maniacal pace through the city streets. He took Balbo over to Lake Shore Drive. Turner had called Ian immediately after roll call. Ian had set up the appointment with Mary Ann Eliot at Ann Sather's Restaurant on the north side, and the reporter requested to be in on it. Turner promised his friend he'd give him a full report later, but didn't think it appropriate for him to be present at this time.

Fenwick pulled off the Drive at Belmont and drove the few blocks to the restaurant. They parked illegally under the el tracks and strode over.

Turner recognized Eliot, although she didn't remember him from the campaign. Having already eaten breakfast with his sons, Turner ordered black coffee. Fenwick slathered several cinnamon rolls with mounds of butter.

The alderman drank black coffee and ordered a plate of fresh fruit.

Mary Ann Eliot was a slender woman with brown hair cut short. She'd draped a beige cloth overcoat over the back of her chair.

Eliot placed her manicured hands around her coffee cup, expressed concern about the difficulty of the case they were working on. Their food arrived promptly. Turner and Fenwick ate and drank while Eliot continued. She pointed at Turner. "Ian said I should trust you. I looked up our campaign records. You did good work in the election."

"Stuffed a few envelopes," Turner said. He told her that they wanted as much background as she could give them on Gideon Giles and his political career.

"The Fifth Ward is different," she said. She gave them a brief history of the ward. Before being annexed to Chicago in various stages in the nineteenth century, the Hyde Park area of the ward was a well-to-do suburb. A major reason for its history of unconventional politics came from the prodigious influence of the University of Chicago. The ward had a long tradition of liberal independent aldermen. "Getting votes for the machine candidate in the Fifth Ward can be difficult."

"What about having a Democratic party committeeman," Fenwick asked.

"The party managed to keep its thumb on the real power. The aldermen could do what they wanted. Party politics at the precinct level was another matter. The party's control wasn't as great in the Fifth Ward as in other places, but it was still there."

"What about the election when Gideon Giles ousted Mike McGee?" Turner asked.

"Mike McGee." She spoke the name wistfully, almost sadly. "I grew up on stories about Mike McGee. He was one of the most loved and hated men in my house. We had regular arguments about him. One time my dad banished my older brother and sister for three months for speaking well of him. My dad had his loyalties and he thought his kids should share them."

"What were the arguments about?" Turner asked.

"Some of it was class-related. McGee was lace-curtain Irish. We were dirt-poor back-of-the-yards. He was also a liberal. He'd oppose the mayor at critical times. Even criticized the first Mayor Daley. My father idolized Dick Daley. In the sixties my dad thought the only thing standing between revolution and anarchy was Richard J. Daley. My dad saw the criticism as betrayal."

"What about yourself?" Turner asked. "How did you see him?"

"I thought McGee was an opportunistic politician like most alderman. Ready to make a buck or a deal. I've never understood him." Eliot herself had gotten a job and put herself through law school, then slaved in democratic precinct politics for a long time. She moved to the 43rd when she realized she'd never get higher up in the patriarchal politics of the southwest side. She wasn't bitter about that. "I understand the people and sympathize with many of their causes. I believe that all politics is local. Pick up the garbage. Get them city services in a timely way. Keep the pot holes filled. My dad's connections got me started in the Forty-third. After the 1991 remap the Forty-third Ward opened up. I ran and won."

"How well did you know Giles?" Turner asked.

"Not very well. I found him offensive. For him everything

had to be shrill, had to be on fast forward, had to be now. He had no sense of compromise. Worse, he didn't have a good sense of what the ward needed. You can cater to the shrill social-welfare crowd only for so long. People in his ward went without because he was an idiot."

"What about beating McGee for committeeman? What happened there?" Turner asked.

"You can have two stories. The current political wisdom or the Irish grapevine."

"I'll take both," Turner said.

Eliot hesitated then said to Turner, "I'll trust you for three reasons. One, Ian set this up, and I trust his judgement. Two, you're gay. Three, after listening to you, I trust you."

Everybody paused, sipped coffee. Eliot continued, "Conventional wisdom. Mike McGee got too old. He offended almost every group in the ward. The black politicians finally got fed up and abandoned him in the primary. If they'd been able to unite in the general election, they could probably have beaten Giles in the runoff."

In Chicago all the candidates run in the same primary regardless of party. If no candidate won fifty percent plus one vote, they had a runoff between the top two vote-getters.

The waitress refilled their coffee cups. When the waitress left, Eliot continued, "The inside gossip says that somebody moved in with a ton of money. Enough to buy off all of Mike McGee's major supporters."

"How did Giles get their support?" Turner asked.

"The Irish grapevine says he had to promise them something," Eliot said, "but I haven't heard what. I've tried to figure it out. He hasn't had a pattern of appointments that raise eyebrows. He hasn't voted for any particular utility or money interest. In fact, he's always against them. He just rants about causes. I figure there's got to be a pattern somewhere. It just hasn't been discovered yet."

"How would we find the pattern?" Fenwick asked.

"I don't know. If some of the wiliest politicians in the city haven't been able to, it could be impossible to find. And it's not for lack of trying. I've heard several aldermen and the mayor's office have had squads of people digging to find his source of money."

"So the guy's very clever," Fenwick said.

"Maybe there's nothing to find," Turner said.

"Got to be," Eliot said. "The idea that somebody got paid-off is too current to be totally false."

"Who could we ask about it?" Turner asked.

"My father," Eliot said.

Turner looked at her over her cup of coffee and raised a quizzical eyebrow.

"Yeah, he has trouble with my being a lesbian. He's also secretly very proud of what I've accomplished. All the other kids in the family have dead-end city jobs. I'm the only one who made a name. He might be able to give you a lead or two."

She used the pay phone to set up the appointment. She came back to the table. "My father's officially retired, but you'll find him in the ward office. Can't keep him away and can't shut him up. Be careful or he'll tell you a million stories of his wild Irish youth in the heart of Chicago's south side."

They thanked her and left. Fenwick and Turner took Lake Shore Drive to the Stevenson Expressway, to the Dan Ryan. Chicago expressways had generally understandable monickers, named for reasonably famous politicians: the Eisenhower, the Kennedy, the Stevenson, and then there was the Dan Ryan. Everybody knew who the first three people were. Nobody knew who Dan Ryan was or how he got an expressway named after him. Old Dan was a relatively obscure party functionary, son of an obscure party functionary. Nothing like loyalty to the old Chicago machine to get you immortalized in concrete.

They took Thirty-fifth Street past the new Comiskey Park

and turned south on Halsted to Exchange. This was the mayor's ward, the Eleventh. They passed frame houses and brick bungalows and numerous aging Roman Catholic churches. The neighborhood came about in the 1830s when Irish immigrants arrived to help construct the Illinois-Michigan Canal. They built houses south of the Chicago River. In those days it was often referred to as "Cabbage Patch," because residents grew cabbage in their gardens. The name changed to "Bridgeport" because a bridge across the river at Ashland Avenue was too low for barges to pass under. Traders would unload on one side of the bridge, and then reload their materials on the other side. Perhaps the most famous part of the neighborhood was the old stockyards. The Union Stock Yards came from a merger in 1865 of many smaller companies. For years, vast herds of cattle, sheep, and pigs set off a memorable stench as they came there to be slaughtered.

The ward office turned out to be an unprepossessing one-story brick building. They walked up to the front counter. People strode about a twenty-by-thirty room with purpose in their steps. Some sat at computer terminals quietly typing. Ringing phones were answered promptly in soft voices. A smiling young woman greeted them cheerfully. She took them to corner room in the rear of the office.

A man behind a large desk rose to greet them. He was immense, tall as well as broad, with white hair and a red face, but when he spoke it was with a soft Irish burr. Brendan Eliot smiled at them. He said, "The alderman said I could use his office this morning. A courtesy to an old man. My daughter spoke most highly of you."

Turner and Fenwick sat in two comfortable leather chairs facing the old man who sat in a high back swivel rocker. The walls were covered with sports bric-a-brac related to the White Sox. Crammed amid the jock heroes were photos of the mayor and the alderman with various politicians, and pictures of the alderman with his family.

While Turner was sure Mary Ann had told her father the purpose of their visit, he went over it again.

"Gideon Giles," Eliot murmured when Turner finished. "A man who could have done a lot for the people of his ward or the city. Never knew how to get things done or get along."

Turner said, "We were wondering about his race with Mike McGee. How did Giles manage to win?"

At the name McGee, Brendan Eliot's face turned nearly purple, but his voice remained soft. He said, "Mike McGee was a traitor. His lace-curtain ways." The sneer in his voice left them no doubt that "lace curtain" was a bad thing to be. He told them of how the "lace curtain" Irish were those who got enough money and moved out of the Eleventh to the Nineteenth Ward, the Morgan Park and Beverly areas. "For years those fools fought us for control of the city. Used to call them 'the Irish turkeys of Beverly.' They lost every time they tried to beat us."

"But McGee was in the Fifth Ward," Fenwick said.

"The man was odd. Never knew what was good for him. His family moved out of the old neighborhood, but old Mike was a bit of the rebel even then. Did you know he graduated summa cum laude from the University of Chicago? Took a lot of money. He had to work very hard. Thought he was better than the rest of us. That independent streak went over real well with all the pointy heads in that neighborhood. We knew him for what he was: shanty Irish trying to thumb his nose at the rest of us. That's why he opposed the mayor when he did. Wanted to cause trouble. I bet he never believed in one of the causes he fought for or against."

"How could Giles have beaten him?" Turner asked.

"Money. Lots of it."

"From where?" Turner asked.

Eliot shrugged. "Somebody had to cut a deal with the other politicians in the ward. Mike McGee had that ward under his belt. He never should have lost."

"Who could tell us where the money came from and who made the deals?" Turner asked.

The old Irishman smiled. Turner's cop instincts told him a lie was coming. What he got was an enormous evasion. Somehow Eliot managed to tell them a fifteen-minute story about his boyhood without revealing another thing about Chicago politics.

In the car Fenwick said, "Charming old liar."

Turner said, "Storyteller is more polite. I think we should at least try the other politicians in the ward. If they abandoned McGee, they might at least tell us why."

"In this city? Getting the truth out of anybody in ward politics is going to be tough."

"Let's try."

They stopped at Area Ten headquarters. Carruthers and Roderiguez weren't around. No one had any other news on the case. None of the other detectives in the Area Ten knew enough about Fifth Ward politics to help them find out who had the real power. They called the Prairie Avenue police district, which included Hyde Park. An old buddy of Fenwick's was a sergeant. Fenwick talked to him for fifteen minutes, scribbling an occasional note.

Fenwick hung up and said, "I got it." He showed Turner a list. "My buddy is fairly sure that these are the most powerful people in the ward."

Turner didn't recognize any of the names.

They took Lake Shore Drive south to Hyde Park. Their first stop was on the west side of Washington Park. They took Fifty-fifth Street to State, then south on State Street, a sharp right on Fifty-seventh, and half a block to their destination. They got out of the car and Turner saw Fenwick pat both of the weapons he carried. The neighborhood wasn't the best and the structure they approached was as unsavory as any in the city. Iron grillwork covered the windows on the first and second floor of a five-story building. Windows within the grillwork had been covered from the inside with uneven boards. Graffiti ran along the graying cement brick facing. Turner recognized some of the gang symbols and identification marks. The upper stories seemed to be mostly intact, but badly in need of a cleaning and a paint job.

Several surly teenagers eyed them suspiciously as they approached the door. The youngsters said nothing and averted their eyes as the cops passed. They swung open the ground-floor door and entered a vestibule. It smelled of disinfectant, and while most of the surfaces were dirt encrusted, someone had obviously tried to keep the trash picked up. New bronze mailboxes gleamed on their left. The address they had indicated a third-floor office. An inner door that may have at one time needed to be opened by a tenant from their apartment, yielded to Turner's twist of the knob.

The first two flights of stairs continued the motif of the entryway, clean and neat but in need of repair.

At the top of the second flight of stairs they met a barrier of newly walled plaster and an unvarnished wooden door.

"This can't be right," Fenwick said. He checked the piece of paper he'd written the address down on, shook his head. "I wrote it right. Can't believe some big-time politician lives or works out of this place."

Turner knocked on the door. They waited through several moments of silence. Turner raised his arm to knock again. The door swung open on silent hinges.

A youthful African-American male in a dark-gray suit, white shirt, and tie greeted them gravely. They showed him their identification, and he moved aside to let them in.

The room they entered took up the entire third floor. Turner could see out the windows on every side to the grey sky outside. A nicked and scarred grand staircase in the center of the room led to the floor above. Around the room people sat at old wooden desks. Turner heard the sounds of computer keys clicking, and a printer to his left scrolled out copy. He saw fax machines and numerous computer screens. Telephones buzzed softly instead of ringing.

Fenwick asked to see Martha Chambers, the person his sergeant contact recommend they start with. The person who opened the door asked them to wait for a moment. He retired to a nearby console, spoke softly into an intercom. He returned and said, "Ms. Chambers will see you now."

"The Chambers name rings a faint bell," Turner murmured as they crossed the room.

Fenwick shrugged. "Doesn't mean anything to me."

The young man led them up the grand staircase. For all the modernity Turner saw around the room, he was struck by a sense of age and permanence. Luxurious Persian area rugs around the room were old and discolored. Prints of early Chicago, one a sketch of Fort Dearborn, were faded in their frames. Up the staircase they found a hallway lined with a rose-colored carpet and with enclosed offices both to left and right. Turner caught glimpses of well-dressed men and women going about their tasks. At the end of the corridor the young man opened a solid oak door.

Turner and Fenwick entered a small room with floor-to-ceiling bookcases along the entire south wall. A window opened to the west. A large map of the city covered the center of the north wall. In the middle of the room two faded velour couches faced each other. Between them was a coffee table made of a wooden door standing on legs of bricks.

A woman Turner guessed to be in her thirties rose to greet them. She shook hands solemnly and indicated they should sit. The young man who led them in exited quietly. Turner explained that they were following leads in the Gideon Giles murder, and that they thought if they could understand the political situation in the ward, they might find someone who might have a motive for murder.

Martha Chambers wore a grey blazer, matching skirt, and white blouse. She nodded gravely and spoke quietly. "I'm not sure how my small business here can help you."

The two detectives sat on the couch facing the window. Ms. Chambers sat on the other.

Turner said, "We understand that powerful political forces pulled out on Mike McGee. We'd like to know why."

"Did you ask Mr. McGee?" she asked.

"He's old, and I think out of touch," Turner said.

"Your analysis is correct," she said. "But why come to me. I'm not a politician."

"A contact gave us your name," Fenwick said.

She smiled. "If you had called, I could have saved you a visit. I have a small business here that has been doing work in the African-American community since my great-grandfather was elected alderman in 1920. He was one of the first African-American alderman in the city. We provide services to those in need: day care, jobs, housing."

"Do you know who might have enough power to sabotage Mike McGee?" Turner asked.

"Sabotage?" she asked. "He simply lost an election."

Fenwick said, "Yes, ma'am, but we're trying to find out why."

"Because his opponent got more votes." Her smile took some of the sting from the comment.

Turner said, "We understand that. We need to check to see if there is a political motive for his murder."

She said, "I'm sorry. We have no political connection. I suggest you try the mayor's office. That's where the political power is in this city, not in my small business here."

As they descended the stairs to the outside door Fenwick said, "This may all look old and outdated, but I bet that woman has more say in this ward than half the politicians. I wonder what's in the rest of this building. It can't just be her 'little business.' I'm suspicious."

Turner sighed. "We'll have to research it when we get back to the station."

They grabbed some lunch and then for the next three hours they drove around the ward visiting a liquor store, an illegal betting parlor, a dry cleaners, and a rib joint, all of whose owners they found on their list of movers and shakers in the ward. At two of them they didn't find the owners in. The others repeated Martha Chambers's words that McGee lost because he was out of touch with his ward, but that none of them had enough connection or power to cause him to lose.

"Double fuck," Fenwick said as they drove north on Martin Luther King Drive back to the station. "They were lying," Fenwick said. "I can feel it."

"What we need is an inside connection in the mayor's office," Turner said.

"Do we know a cop who has access?"

"I don't," Turner said. "Depends on how bad people really want this case solved. We can ask the commander when we get back."

At Area Ten headquarters they talked to uniformed officers checking the backgrounds of: all the people connected with Giles's campaign staff, everyone connected with Giles's private life, anyone who knew Frank Ricken. They'd given them a cramped section of a fourth-floor storage area for the team working on the case. Turner sat on a pile of cardboard boxes as he talked to the senior staff officers working the computer checks and phone calls. Fenwick went in search of the commander to find a contact in the mayor's office.

Turner asked what they had so far.

Jack Blessing, an African-American cop in his late twenties, told him, "We've gone through nearly 500 people. We have enough unpaid parking tickets among these political people to pay off the national debt. One of the campaign staff got caught for shoplifting in Des Moines, Iowa, in 1962." He flipped through several pages of notebook. "Most everybody working the campaign comes up with nothing. We've got five or six arrested at various demonstrations from the late sixties to last year." He showed Turner the list of names.

Turner didn't recognize any of them.

"Did you start on the ward organization as well as all the reform organizations he was involved in?" Turner asked.

Blessing frowned. "You're not serious."

Turner nodded.

"We'll add them to the list," Blessing said dejectedly.

"How about Ricken's people?"

"Nothing on the family. Brother and sister in Indiana, both schoolteachers. Mom and dad retired and living in Centerboro, little suburb outside Aurora. We're hunting through friends."

"You get anything on those University people, especially Sorenson, Worthington, and Kempe?"

Blessing checked through a stack of papers, read for a second, and said, "They're all clean. Hardly a parking ticket among the three of them."

The probability of any of the background information giving them a substantial clue was about the same as winning the lottery or getting struck by lightning, but it had to be done. Some profile or pattern might be found.

"Rodriguez and Carruthers back from checking into the liberal groups?" Turner asked.

"Haven't seen them," Blessing said.

Turner walked down to his desk on the third floor. He leaned his elbows on the top and cupped his chin in his hands. Fenwick swung into the room before he had a chance to reflect on what they learned.

"I got us an interview with a third–deputy assistant mayor in charge of snowing the public," Fenwick said.

"Why bother?" Turner said.

"Commander set it up. Shows the mayor's office is trying to help. We've got fifteen minutes to get to the interview."

Fenwick squeezed through Loop traffic and parked illegally on Clark Street across from City Hall.

The third–deputy assistant mayor took ten minutes to tell them how cooperative the mayor's office planned to be.

Turner asked about politics in the Fifth Ward and who had the power to overthrow Mike McGee.

The third–deputy assistant mayor took twenty more minutes to explain how the mayor's office didn't get involved in local ward politics.

Turner put a restraining hand on Fenwick's arm. His partner hadn't said anything, but Turner recognized the signs. Fenwick was close to blowing when he started rolling up the sides of the paper in his notebook. When Fenwick snapped his pen in two between his fingers the third–deputy assistant mayor said, "Is something wrong?"

Turner said quickly, "Thank you for your help," and got Fenwick out of the room as quickly as possible.

"Double fuck, triple fuck, asshole dumb numbnuts son of a bitch shit for brains." Fenwick raged through the outer offices all the way to the car. Numerous office workers and then pedestrians stared after him.

In the car Turner said, "Did the commander explain why we needed to talk to this particular guy?"

"Huh?" Fenwick said.

"You were sitting there when the commander called?"

Fenwick nodded.

"Did he tell the guy on the other end that we thought ward politics might be the motivation for the murder."

Fenwick gazed at him thoughtfully. "I think he said something about people in the ward maybe being behind the murder."

"Geared to warn even the densest politician," Turner said.

"Are you saying we can't trust the commander?" Fenwick said.

"Not ready to go that far. He may have given too much

9 5

information. The people at City Hall aren't stupid. We've got to talk to politically connected people."

"We could try Mary Ann Eliot again," Fenwick said.

The police radio called their car number. Turner acknowledged.

The dispatcher said, "We've got another problem for you."

F I V E

Turner and Fenwick walked into the Fifth Ward office. Uniformed cops outside, tech personnel inside, static from cop radios, people murmuring back and forth to each other, and blood on the floor as they crossed the threshold. Speckles of blood at irregular intervals lead to the back room. On the rear wall of the former alderman's office, handprints of red streaked down two of the posters, which now featured bloody whales and smeared wetlands. Surrounded by paramedics, Jack Stimpson, the media consultant, slumped in the desk chair. Bandages covered the left side of his head.

Turner spoke to the uniformed cop who showed up first, Miriam Blackwell, in her early twenties, blond hair in a pony tail. She chewed on her gum for a minute then responded to Turner's question.

"Call came in about fifteen minutes ago. Guy next door was

washing pots in the restaurant. Heard shouts then a couple of pops. Said he knew the sound of gunfire. Called it in. We got here, door was open, neighbors gawking outside. Claim nobody walked in here." She checked her notebook. "We saw the blood. Called the tech people immediately. Found this guy on the floor in here." She pointed to Stimpson. "Refuses to go to a hospital. Not shot, but beat-up pretty bad."

"Why not crawl out to the street for help? Why'd he come back here?" Turner asked.

"Have to ask him," she said.

Fenwick jerked a thumb toward the outer office. "Anybody out there see anything?"

"Nothing yet. We've got the names down. We're trying to keep everybody in the crowd here." She left.

The paramedics finished their work, suggested Stimpson see a doctor. He shook his head. They left.

Turner sat on the desk. Stimpson looked at him through eyes rapidly purpling. "What happened?" Turner asked.

"I was working. Trying to clean out my files. My work here was done. Three men burst in here with nylon stockings over their heads. They didn't say anything. I thought it was a robbery, but they simply started beating me. I thought I was going to die."

"Why'd they stop?" Fenwick asked.

"I don't know. They shot a gun off into the wall and ran out."

"No one else here today?" Turner asked.

"No. I think most everybody went home early. I waited until after the wake started this afternoon to come in."

"Why crawl back here?" Turner asked.

"I was afraid they'd be waiting for me out in the street. I managed to get to the desk, but I must have passed out. I don't remember anything else until the police came."

"Why attack you?" Fenwick asked.

"I don't know. It was awful."

They asked more questions but got few answers. Finally Stimpson said, "I can't take any more of this. I'd like to leave now."

A few minutes later he was led out by a campaign staffer who lived in the neighborhood.

"Why this campaign organization?" Fenwick asked.

"Murder's got to be connected to these attacks," Turner said. "Who'd they piss off? Who gains by harming these people?"

"Doesn't make sense," Fenwick said. "Murder a Chicago alderman and who cares? Doesn't affect the political life of the world much. And as a group, one Chicago alderman more or less is not a huge loss."

Turner knew Fenwick's attitude reflected the jaded opinion of Chicagoans toward their city council members more than heartlessness.

"Has to be something more personal," Fenwick concluded.

Turner nodded agreement. "And why murder Giles and only attack these guys? What do they know or don't they know that's keeping them alive?"

"We only think Ricken's still alive," Fenwick said. "Or at least he hasn't turned up dead yet."

Turner said, "We've got to check into their campaign activities, and we've got to find somebody who's an expert on all these groups they belonged to."

"Don't know where we're going to find any more sources," Fenwick said. "So far what we've tried has turned to shit."

"We've got too many people. We've got to begin narrowing this down."

The commander walked in. "Hell of a mess," he said.

Fenwick said, "We got shit from that idiot you sent us to in city hall."

One of these days Fenwick's bluntness was going to cause a big problem, Turner thought.

Turner explained what had happened at City Hall.

"My contacts at City Hall aren't the best," the commander said. "I agree with Buck's assessment. You got shit. Sorry. If they're stonewalling, we've got political problems. This case was screwed up enough before." He harrumphed. "I'll try a few other contacts. I don't have a lot of hope."

Turner knew the stories about the commander. He had too much skill to be kept out of top positions, but he lacked political backing. He had no clout pushing for him behind the sidelines, and if you didn't have major clout behind you in Chicago, you had to have stupendous skills to move up past the functionaries that filled city offices.

"What happened here?" the commander asked.

They explained. The commander agreed the murder, Ricken's disappearance, and the beating here had to be connected. Instead of his usual few words of encouragement, he pressed them to come up with a solution. "The press is nuts on this, and whether City Hall wants to help or not, they are saying all the right thing to show excessive concern. I need answers." He left minutes later. Turner has never seen him look this worried.

Turner and Fenwick talked to witnesses. They called Mable Ashcroft, the alderman's chief assistant, who came to the office and went over the list of socially concerned organizations in which Giles and his people had been involved. They dropped the list off at Area Ten headquarters. On the fourth floor Turner told Blessing to have his people check all of the organizations for anything remotely illegal or any connection to violence.

Back at his desk, Turner found the report from the crime lab. He scanned it quickly. In the fingerprint section, he found what he suspected, the half-opened bottle of homemade vegetable brew had only Giles's fingerprints on it. The other bottles included Giles's and some random prints, probably from a store clerk. If the murderer had touched them, the prints would probably have been rubbed off them as well. Still they'd try and check them out.

Fingerprinting as a method of solving a case was highly overrated. Unless you had a suspect to match them up with, it was virtually impossible to check the ones you had against every fingerprint on file in Chicago, much less with the FBI or any other criminal jurisdiction. Once you had a suspect, they were excellent for confirming if the criminal was there or not. Richard Speck, who killed eight student nurses in Chicago, left one clear print at the scene. On a door the print was eighteen inches off the ground, a place cops didn't normally check, but the case was so horrific, they'd checked the entire door, and they did find it, and they got him.

It was midnight before Turner got out of the station. He'd called home around six. Brian and Jeff were in, since it was a school night. They'd eaten at Mrs. Talucci's. Brian would have made sure Jeff got to bed on time. Paul pulled into his driveway, turned off the ignition, and listened to the murmurs and clicks of the car settling to rest for the night. He heard traffic on Taylor Street nearby, a horn honked, a siren clanged in the distance. He looked toward Mrs. Talucci's house. The lights in the back half of the ground floor gleamed softly through the windows. Paul glanced in, but didn't see Mrs. Talucci. Knitting lay sprawled on the kitchen table. He knew she must be upset, because she hated knitting. She thought it was for old fuddy-duddies who didn't have anything better to do with their lives. He considered stopping in for a visit.

He opened the car door, began to get out, then reached back for his briefcase. A shot rang through the night. The glass in the driver's side window shattered. Paul scrambled out of the car and flattened himself on the ground. He peered between the wheels of the car trying to see where the shot came from.

The window in his house six feet above him slid open.

Turner could make out Mrs. Talucci's and Brian's face in the opening.

"Get back," Paul whispered.

The two heads disappeared. Paul crawled behind his car, dashed across the two feet to the back of his house and in the back door.

Brian and Mrs. Talucci met him in the kitchen.

"I've got to call this in," Paul said.

"They'll be here in a few seconds," Mrs. Talucci said.

Minutes later three squad cars screeched to a halt out front, another rolled into the alley in the back. Two unmarked cars blocked the street.

Mrs. Talucci joined Paul on the front porch, talking to the cops. Lights went on in a few houses on the street. Mrs. Talucci told the officers to keep their voices down so as not to waken the neighborhood, so the men and women of the department spent most of the time whispering in deference to Mrs. Talucci's commands. Two of the uniforms hunted in back where they thought the shot had come from.

They came back ten minutes later. Reported they hadn't found anything. They promised to return in the daylight to continue the search. Finally the police left and the neighborhood returned to normal.

Mrs. Talucci joined Brian and Paul in their kitchen. While Paul put together a late supper, Mrs. Talucci explained that minutes before Paul drove up, she and Brian had both thought they heard someone sneaking through their connected backyards.

Brian said, "I turned on the back porch light and went outside. Mrs. Talucci told me to douse the light and get back inside. She joined me here. Then you drove up. I checked Jeff. He slept through the whole thing."

They discussed the gunshot, and Paul told them about the case. Mrs. Talucci was firmly convinced the shot fired was an attack related to the investigation.

Paul remained doubtful but didn't contradict her.

Mrs. Talucci said, "I didn't remember the other day when we first talked about it, but I attended a lecture by Gideon Giles when I was at the University." Mrs. Talucci had gotten her masters degree in philosophy from the University of Chicago while she was in her seventies. "A fool," she declared. "He spoke at some esoteric cross-discipline forum. Supposed to be about philosophy and language. He talked about some cause or other."

"Off the topic?" Paul said.

"Just plain stupid," she said, "and I didn't like him. He smiled like a politician who's been stealing from the till."

"Most of his campaign staff said he was honest and upright. Couple of the politicians claimed he had to have sold out, but we've got no proof of that."

Mrs. Talucci said, "I've lived in this city all my life. I've read the papers. I've listened in the neighborhood. I know when somebody's sold out to win an election. Mike McGee should never have lost."

"Who would Giles sell out to?" Turner asked.

"Who's benefited the most since he's been in the council?" she replied.

"I don't know."

She patted him on the shoulder. "It'll take hard work. It's late now and you need some sleep. I'll talk to a few people."

Turner was never quite sure about Mrs. Talucci's connections. Her "talking to people" could mean anything from being connected to the most powerful mafia don in the country to gossiping with the neighbors. Often amazing things seemed to get done when Mrs. Talucci talked to people. Several years ago a gang of street kids had been harassing older women returning from the Jewel grocery store on Harrison Street. One of the kids had been found hanging naked upside down from the front of the store the day after Mrs. Talucci had "talked to someone." The problems at the store never recurred. The kid was fine but never said a word about who attacked him.

Paul stopped at Jeff's bedroom downstairs before going up. He pulled his son's tangled sheet up over the slender body against the early morning coolness. He sat on the edge of the bed and watched the boy breathe quietly. He touched the sleeping boy's check. Jeff sighed and opened his eyes.

"Hi, Dad," he said sleepily.

"Go back to sleep, son," Paul said.

"I love you," Jeff said.

Paul leaned over and kissed his son's forehead. "I love you, son," he said. The boy sighed and moments later was fast asleep.

The next morning Brian stumbled into the kitchen, took one look at Paul and said, "You look like hell, Dad."

Jeff swung in on his crutches, plopped himself at his place, and opened his math book. He wanted help with some homework.

"Why didn't you ask your brother last night?" Paul asked.

"I tried to help him," Brian said.

"You explain it better, Dad" Jeff said. "And I missed you. I wanted you to be home."

This was familiar territory to most cops. Their high divorce rate was a testimony to how the time demanded by their jobs affected them. Paul soothed and cuddled his younger son for an extra fifteen minutes and slipped into the squad room late for roll call.

When they finished, Turner organized the team for the day. Background checks needed to be finished. Fingerprint reports needed to be gone over. Turner held out little hope for either task being of real help. Paperwork on people interviewed needed to be completed. Plus they had more interviews to conduct.

"We need to investigate the poison and the vegetable juice," Turner said.

"Taste probably disguised the poison," Fenwick said. "Don't know how anybody can drink that shit."

"We can try to find out where he bought the stuff," Turner said. "Might give us a clue."

Turner called Laura Giles to see if she knew where her husband bought his juice and ingredients. She sounded groggy. Turner gave her a few minutes to wake up. When he asked his question again she said, "I have no idea. I told you I knew he was into health foods. I don't know anything else."

Turner called Ian at nine. His friend picked up the phone on the seventh ring and said, "This better be fucking important."

"I have the scoop of the century for you," Turner said.

"I don't care. I was up late trying to seduce a twenty-one-year-old college student. The sniveling little creep strung me along for three hours, then claimed he had to go to his parents' home and study for an exam today."

"I'm sure you were talking to him in the name of doing vital research," Turner said.

"Goddamn wrong. Kid was bright, articulate, witty, and cute."

"I'd be happy to discuss your love life," Turner said, "but I'm trying to catch a murderer."

"I almost murdered the little creep last night," Ian said.

"I need to talk about reform organizations and who's got what power in the city. I need to talk to Mary Ann Eliot again. I thought we might set it up for the same time."

Ian grumbled, but Turner told him he could sit in this time as long as the whole thing remained off the record. They agreed to meet for lunch.

Fenwick came up to Turner's desk and said, "I've got the address of Jack Stimpson, the media consultant. That fucker was lying last night. He knew more than he told. I want to put some pressure on him."

They drove to the north side address. Jack Stimpson and his wife lived in one of the trendiest and most expensive sections of Lincoln Park, on Fullerton Avenue just west of Clark.

Fenwick was pissed about the shot fired at Turner the night before. As they drove up Wells Street, he said, "Why the fuck would they shoot at you? How did they find out where you lived? And is it connected to this shit-ass investigation? And why?"

"You asked all that already," Turner said.

"Double fuck," Fenwick said.

"No matter how many fucks it is," Turner said, "we have no way of proving anything now. You know how this is going to go. We have this huge task force of a zillion people. It'll stay in the headlines, probably for a good while, because these people are prominent. If we get lucky, one of these millions of useless facts will lead to a miniscule connection. So far we've got very little besides one dead body, one missing person, and one attack."

"What about that kid's room at the university?" Fenwick asked.

"That might be connected. I don't know. What I do know is whoever did all this has covered their tracks pretty goddamn well."

"I'm worried about the attack on you," Fenwick said.

"I've got my vest on." Regulations didn't yet require detectives on the Chicago police force to wear bulletproof vests. All uniformed officers were required to and many wore them. "And I can't post twenty-four-hour guards on the kids. The neighborhood has been alerted and Mrs. Talucci said she'd talk to a few people."

"If I was in a fight, I'd rather have Mrs. Talucci on my side than half the cops in the city," Fenwick said.

At the Stimpsons a butler met them at the front door. They identified themselves and said they wanted to speak to Stimpson. The butler asked them to wait and shut the door.

Fenwick said, "I've never seen a guy in a tuxedo except at weddings. Never been to a place that had a butler either. I guess that happens when you deal with a better class of murderer."

The butler returned a few moments later to usher them into the front hall. Hardwood floors that looked to have been polished that morning, and a ceiling that soared three floors to a massive silver chandelier.

Jack Stimpson entered the room a few minutes later. He still had bandages on his head. He sat stiffly as if his ribs hurt. A woman entered the room and stood behind him. She wore a black dress, no jewelry, and little makeup. Turner and Fenwick rose.

Stimpson introduced her as his wife Melissa. She remained standing while the others sat.

"I talked to you last night," Stimpson said.

"We need to get to the bottom of what's going on," Turner said. "We need your help."

"We can't help," Melissa Stimpson said. "I told Jack we should never have gotten involved in local Chicago politics. We've done large media campaigns for national organizations. This city has such an awful political reputation. We know nothing about these people."

Turner said, "Maybe you could help me understand a few things." Before either of them could object he continued. "Are you saying that Gideon Giles could afford to pay you on the same scale as a national campaign?"

"We work in many campaigns. Usually not something as small as a local aldermanic election, but we've done it."

"Didn't you wonder where he could get the kind of money to afford you?" Fenwick asked.

"The checks never bounced," Stimpson said. "The payments were always on time. You never know which campaigns will make the most money."

"Did you work closely with any of the liberal causes Giles championed?" Turner asked.

"No. I was mostly involved with the campaign staff."

"You know Ricken was attacked and is now missing?" Fenwick said. "We think the attacks and the murder are connected."

Neither Stimpson spoke.

Turner asked softly, "What did your attackers say to you last night, Mr. Stimpson?"

Stimpson glared at the two detectives. Mrs. Stimpson put her hand on her husband's shoulder. "They said nothing," he said.

"Did you know them?" Fenwick asked.

"No. I told you that last night."

"Why don't you leave us alone," Mrs. Stimpson said. "My husband told you all he knew. Go away."

Politicians had fought to have Jack Stimpson be their media guru. He rarely backed losers and had a reputation for only supporting people whose politics he believed in, as opposed to the usual stereotype of the media consultant selling out to the highest bidder. Now here was this national figure lying through his teeth, and his wife helping in the cover-up. They must be frightened; of whom and why is what Turner wanted to know.

"Can't go away, ma'am," Fenwick said. "This is part of a murder investigation. Can't stop until we know everything."

Stimpson said, "The only one in the organization people fought with was Frank Ricken. Maybe it was the murderer who attacked him, and now that's he's missing, maybe the killer got to him and dumped his body somewhere. I know for sure Frank wasn't one of those who attacked me last night."

The detectives left a few minutes later.

"Frightened," Fenwick said in the car. "Scared out of their minds."

Turner agreed. "But by whom? And why?"

Fenwick shrugged.

At eleven-thirty, they met Ian Hume and Mary Ann Eliot at the Melrose Restaurant on Broadway. They sat in a back booth away from the early lunchtime crowd. Mary Ann Eliot wore a black blazer, a gray skirt, and white blouse. Ian wore his slouch fedora, which he did not take off even for meals. At six-foot-six with bright red hair, Ian stood out in any crowd. Other than the hat his sartorial splendor was muted. Today he wore black pleated pants, a white shirt, and a Chicago Cubs warm-up jacket.

The waitress brought coffee. They ordered lunch. Turner explained what'd happened the day before when they followed Mary Ann's leads.

"I'm stunned," she said. "My father was definitely covering up."

"Could you get him to tell us more?" Fenwick asked.

She shook her head. "I doubt it. The old boy network is pretty much tottering these days, but it's still clannish and closed to those who aren't in. I doubt if I can do anything to help you there, but I thought you'd get more information from him. I wish I'd known you were going to visit Martha Chambers. I know her extremely well. If you want to go back there, I'll go with you."

"That'll help?" Fenwick asked.

"It should. She and I have worked together for years now. You're white males. That may have been the problem."

"What is that place really?" Fenwick asked.

"You mean the building that houses her organization?" Eliot asked.

Fenwick nodded.

"It's exactly what it purports to be," Eliot said. "She's absolutely trustworthy and a good friend."

Turner said, "What about the election when Giles beat the committeeman, McGee. We keep hearing about mysterious deals and shifts of power as if we had some kind of banana republic coup against him. How do we find out what the hell was going on?"

Mary Ann shook her head. "Since the first Mayor Daley, some of the committeemen have lost power. Their strength was in providing jobs and services to the people in the ward. The position of Fifth Ward boss didn't have a lot of power, but Mike McGee shouldn't have lost."

"So you told us yesterday," Fenwick said. "That's what everybody says, but nobody can tell us what deal Gideon Giles made or who with."

"You've got to offer people something," Ian said. "Money, power, influence, position. Politics is built on who's going to do me some good."

"So who's got all kinds of good done for them since Giles got elected?" Turner asked. "No one so far has any facts on any secret contract deals, skimming money, or buying land based on inside information."

"Maybe somebody realized he wasn't corrupt, couldn't believe such a thing of a Chicago alderman, and decided to revoke his alderman ID," Ian said.

Being an indicted or convicted Chicago alderman was hardly news. Often indicted and frequently convicted of pastimes, which included bribery, extortion, mail fraud, or income tax evasion, seventeen of them have been convicted since 1972 on any number of corruption charges. The voters seldom threw the bums out. Better to know the local crook than to have him or her sneaking around behind your back. That Giles wasn't corrupt was one of his big selling points.

Ian said, "Frankly I find it refreshing to hear that the creep was on the take."

"I thought you liked him," Turner said. "He supported a lot of issues you worked for."

"I liked his support on the issues. Him I could do without. Listening to him for more than two minutes was like being beaten to death with an all-day sucker. He was always up, always hopeful, and all those teeth in his goddamn smile needed to be shoved down his throat."

Mary Ann Eliot said, "I can try some old friends in the 11th Ward. They may know of some connection I'm not aware of. I'll make a few calls before we go to the South Side."

After their sandwiches arrived, Turner asked Ian about the reform groups in the city.

"You don't know the impossibility about what you're asking. You start with all the religious crowd, move to the hot topics of the moment, like the homeless. Then you've got all the human rights activists. You've got pro- and anti-cop groups. South Africa's been big for a while. Add your endangered animals and plants . . ."

"Endangered plants?" Fenwick asked.

"Who knows when someone might pull up the last showy lady slipper in Wauconda Bog?" Ian asked.

"Wauconda Bog?" Turner asked.

"I did an article about them a couple years ago connected with how gay groups could network with other rights causes. How other reformers got things done. I do an article, I remember this shit. Besides the guy in charge of the 'save the lady slipper' crowd was young, sexy, and gorgeous. I found all kinds of excuses to call him. Plus I got myself onto some of their mailing lists. I'm still on them. Once they've got you, they never let go."

"Any of them violent?" Fenwick asked.

"They write letters, call press conferences, try to get media exposure. Not a lot of machine gun–toting environmental terrorists. Most of them are middle-class do-good liberals."

"No violence?" Fenwick asked.

Ian thought. "I've never met any I thought would do anything more violent than smash a cockroach, and a few of the groups not even that much. I could try and find out which ones were most connected with Giles. What have you found among his papers?"

"Lots of shit from every group," Fenwick said, "but nothing that shows tons of money flooding in."

"Most of those groups don't have a lot of money," Mary Ann said, "and most of them don't bother with Chicago alderman."

"He had a shitload of posters up from these groups," Fenwick said.

"Collecting posters is fairly easy," Ian said. "What we need to find out is if he had any money coming in from any of them."

"Or any large sums going to some of them," Turner said.

They dropped Ian at the Gay Tribune offices and then stopped by the alderman's office. She left them to make a few calls. When she came back she said, "Let's try Martha Chambers first."

"Did you get any results on Irish political power?" Turner asked.

"I called in some heavy markers to try and get people to talk," she said. "As soon as I said a word about the murder, people got real quiet real quick." She pointed at Turner and said, "Several people mentioned the attack on you. Word is on the street that you are not a popular man."

"I don't get it," Turner said. "I'm just a cop investigating a murder."

"Nothing is just anything in this town when it comes to politics," Mary Ann said. "Whoever was secretly supporting Giles has to be worried."

"We don't even know if someone was doing something illegal to get him elected," Fenwick said.

"Doesn't have to be illegal," Mary Ann said. "Somebody

who is powerful might not want his support for Gideon Giles to get out. Double-dealing is a well-practiced art in this city, and violence is not unknown as a way of solving a potential political embarrassment."

"Killing me would affect the politics in this city?" Turner asked.

"What you might find out could," Mary Ann said. "Don't take this wrong, but you probably aren't what's important, but what you might find out is. That shot could simply have been a warning to be careful. A note saying keep your mouth shut if you find out something incriminating."

Together they drove to the south side. Outside the five-story building, Mary Ann Eliot ignored the glass that crunched underfoot, the pavement crumbling beneath her, and the surly teenagers who stepped aside as she marched to the door. The same gentleman who greeted them yesterday smiled at Mary Ann Eliot but frowned when he caught sight of the two cops. He ushered them up the grand staircase and to the solid oak door at the end of the corridor.

Martha Chambers and Mary Ann Eliot exchanged hugs and murmured, "It's been too long." Finally seated, Mary Ann explained their business.

Chambers said, "I talked to them yesterday. If I'd known you knew Mary Ann, I would have been kinder."

"This is a murder investigation," Fenwick said. "Withholding information in a case like this is illegal."

She wagged a finger at him. "I didn't say I knew anything yesterday. I said I'd have been kinder. Today I know something. Mary Ann's presence makes it that much easier for me to want to help you."

Fenwick returned her stern gaze. "We're just trying to do a job," he said.

She broke off the stare and sighed. "Yes, I suppose you are." She straightened the lapels of her jacket, sat up erect in her chair, and folded her hands on top of the blotter in the center of her desk. She said, "The Fifth Ward should have had a black alderman many years ago. Partly it's inertia. Partly the liberals who represented us always voted our way. Lot of reasons. Then this guy Giles came along. A lot of minority politicians had been looking forward to the day Mike McGee stepped down. We thought we'd have our big chance."

"Why not run against him?" Fenwick asked.

"It's a lot easier not to run against an entrenched incumbent," Mary Ann said.

"And he'd done a lot of good for this ward," Martha added then continued, "When Giles came around, none of us in the old guard supported him. We may not have been in love with Mike McGee, but he was okay. We saw the election of Gideon Giles as a roadblock. Then money and jobs started drying up for those who supported McGee."

"Who cut the jobs?" Turner asked.

"City Hall. Politicians don't control jobs the way they used to in this town, but believe me, paying back those who support you is still a big-time business. Mike McGee could no longer pay back. He could no longer serve as clout for anybody. A group of us called on him to find out what was wrong. He seemed as confused as the rest of us. The decision had to be coming from City Hall."

"We got nowhere talking to somebody at City Hall yesterday," Fenwick said.

"Who'd you talk to?" Mary Ann asked.

They told her.

"He's a nobody," Mary Ann said.

"I don't get it," Fenwick said. "I thought Mike McGee was on the outs with the big-time politicians in this town."

"Mike knew his place," Martha Chambers said. "He never went so far that they stripped him of his patronage. He could talk a good line in the press, but he was careful never to alienate anyone when it counted."

"Do either of you have a solid contact at City Hall who could give us information?" Turner asked.

Both hesitated then shook their heads. Mary Ann said, "I could check some sources, but I don't think I know anybody that high up who could make decisions like this."

"I don't at all," Martha said. "Are you sure the murder is contacted to Giles winning the alderman's or the committeeman's race?"

"No," Turner said. "It's something we haven't been able to get decent answers to, so we're suspicious, but it doesn't have to be connected. Could simply be the politicians in this city being secretive and sneaky with no particular criminal intent behind it."

"Working behind closed doors is a time-honored tradition in this city," Mary Ann said. "Wouldn't be odd for them to keep things quiet just for the hell of it."

"So people lost jobs," Fenwick said, "but why did the support dry up?"

"No jobs, no loyalty is part of it. The ward still runs on who can get what done. But Gideon Giles started spending money, lots of it. He bought advertising in the black community. He paid volunteers in the black community. He hired an army of people to make phone calls, stuff envelopes, ring doorbells. He paid for a whole precinct organization almost all of whom came from the black community. People saw that and liked it."

"That would take a huge amount of money," Mary Ann said.

"Why so?" Fenwick asked.

Mary Ann said, "Normally your precinct workers either come from your loyal supporters or people who are in some way on the city payroll. Many of them have been there for years. Many of those campaign workers by night are deep in the streets and sanitation department by day, but McGee would have had most of those wrapped up."

"Giles recruited new people by the hundreds," Martha said. "The old cliché of an army of volunteer workers was almost true in his case, only he did it with tons of money."

"Who'd he get it from?" Turner asked. "We keep asking that question. Who was behind him and why? Who benefited?"

The four of them stared at each other.

"Follow the money," Fenwick said. "We'll have to have somebody go over his campaign finances."

"Everybody goes over those disclosure forms these days," Mary Ann said. "If there'd been something suspicious, surely the press would have found it."

"Obviously not," Fenwick said. "We'll check through it all just in case something develops."

The cops thanked them for their help and left. Mary Ann wanted to stay on and visit with her friend.

In the car they called the station to find out if Roosevelt and Wilson had anything new on Ricken. The dispatcher told them to meet the two cops at John Chester's bar, one of the most frequented cop bars in the city. The bar sat on lower Wacker Drive where it would have met Madison Street if it had been upper Wacker Drive.

Fenwick parked the car in the dimness, and they walked to the door. The sinister depths created by the tunnel-like effect of the street held little fear for patrons. The bar's reputation kept possible problems in other parts of the city.

John Chester kept the outside immaculately clean, the sidewalk swept, the picture window washed at least once a day on the outside. The room opened out to the left. Rare patrons complained about the dark gloominess of the interior until they glimpsed the mural painted over the left-hand wall from the front all the way to the back. It looked like an Italian Baroque nightmare. Cherubs and praying nuns abounded on hills and fields, amid enough animals to stock half the zoos in the world. More then one drunk had added splashes of color to corners and crevices of the painting, so that parts had faded erratically.

Those in the know ignored the decor and watched the patrons. If they observed carefully, they would see a procession of local, state, and national politicians. One might stop first in the Chicago mayor's office to get an endorsement, but one always stopped at John Chester's in the hope Chester would give his nod of approval. Years ago he'd been elected alderman in a huge landslide, and then quit four years later to open the bar. One of the few probably honest politicians in the city, he quit to keep his integrity. Most candidates walked away from his bar unendorsed and disappointed. The few upon whom he conferred approval cherished the moment. John Chester hadn't backed a loser in sixteen years.

Turner and Fenwick picked up beers at the bar and joined Wilson and Roosevelt in a booth at the back.

Wilson pointed at Turner. "Your buddy Carruthers came to us with a big secret today," Wilson said. She laughed.

"He's not my buddy," Turner said.

"Told us you were gay," Roosevelt said.

Wilson said, "We told him that the entire squad was gay. That the city had an affirmative-action program for Area Ten. That was funny enough, but then I told him that we'd all assumed he was gay too. Poor guy is in total shock. His mouth was open so wide, I expected his tonsils to fall out." They chuckled over this.

Turner asked about the case.

Roosevelt filled them in. "We talked to Ricken's parents. According to them Frank told them about big problems in the campaign organization. Claims their son said they had huge divisions and big fights."

"What about?" Turner asked.

"Strategy and tactics. Being politically correct or expedient. Getting something accomplished or being ideologically pure.

Ricken claimed that members of the organization were close to being the thought police and that no one could ever get anything done because they were blind to the way politics really worked."

"Fights like that aren't unusual, are they?" Fenwick asked.

Wilson said, "Half the do-good groups in the city have that happen. Never accomplish anything because they can't get off their philosophical butts, but I think it's a little more subtle than what Rosey said." Only Wilson ever called her partner "Rosey." Carruthers tried it once and Wilson picked him up by the front of his shirt and waltzed him backwards across the squad room. It was her pet name for him, and Roosevelt didn't seem to mind.

"We got our own philosopher," Fenwick said.

"Have I threatened to rip your tongue out yet this week?" Wilson asked.

"Only once and you said you didn't have your iron tongs with you. That's the way I prefer having my tongue ripped out," Fenwick said.

"You may get your wish sooner than you think," Wilson said. "Back to the point. I've seen it happen in a few of the groups I belonged to when I was a kid." She glared at Fenwick. "You will not comment on how long ago that was."

"Me?" Fenwick's attempt to look innocent didn't quite work.

Wilson continued, "The members argue for hours about philosophy. You fight about how to do things and why. Today it's also a lot of debate about being politically correct, but I see that as an extra layer beyond what I'm talking about, although I suppose any of it is equally good at paralyzing groups."

"So nobody got anything done and Ricken was angry about it," Turner said.

"More," Roosevelt said, "his parents claimed he told them that Giles had slowly gotten rid of people who got things done over the past six months. They say Ricken confronted Giles about it."

Roosevelt described what the parents had told him. Ricken stormed into the office and confronted Giles with the information. Supposedly that's what the big ruckus was the other day and that's why Ricken was fired.

"Ricken had figured something out," Turner said. "Information that was enough for him to get beat-up, run away, or get killed. We've got to lean on all those campaign people."

"And find all the people who got fired in the past six months, hell the past year," Fenwick said. "Not that we had enough people to interrogate already."

Turner had a thought as they walked toward the door. He pulled Fenwick aside. "I'm going to ask John Chester if he can find anything out about the politics of all this."

"You think he'll help?" Fenwick asked.

"We aren't friends but at least I can ask him. We're desperate enough. What could it hurt?"

Turner asked Chester if he could speak with him privately. They sat in a booth in the back. Turner explained what he needed.

At the end Chester shook his head. "I don't know much about the politics in the Fifth Ward. I'll ask for you, but I can't promise anything."

Turner asked him to do what he could.

At three-thirty, Turner and Fenwick walked into the Fifth Ward offices. Audrey, the receptionist he'd interviewed the other night, greeted them. Turner saw that her eyes were still red from weeping for the recently deceased.

She greeted them by saying, "This place is a mess." She pulled out a tissue and blew her nose. "Gideon dead, Frank missing, Jack beat-up. I tried to stay at the wake to comfort Laura, but I couldn't. I just don't believe all this." She waved a hand at the mass of clutter on top of her desk. "This is all so useless."

Fenwick picked up a couple of the papers on the desk. "What are these?" he asked.

"Telegrams, notes, messages from all the groups we ever helped. From politicians, even from foreign countries. Gideon was known everywhere and now he's gone." Tears escaped her lids.

Five or six people in the office stared at them. Hank, the legislative assistant, walked over. He saw Audrey and suggested she take a break. Audrey walked to the ladies' room and slipped inside.

Hank said, "It's been a rough time for all of us."

His eyes too looked bloodshot from lack of sleep and recovering from the tragedy.

"We need to talk to everybody," Fenwick said.

Hank said, "It's terrible that you haven't been able to catch anyone. We can't figure out why somebody picked this organization to terrorize. Everybody's scared. We wanted to get a full crew in here today, but most everybody is too frightened. People are afraid they might be next."

Turner said, "You didn't tell me Frank Ricken was unpopular the other night when I interviewed you."

"You asked about fights. I didn't know they fought."

"Why was he unpopular?" Turner asked.

"The women hated—well, that's too strong a word, disliked him a lot. He'd ask them for dates, and he'd be pretty ugly about it if he got turned down. He thought he was god's gift to the female."

"What do you mean, 'He got ugly'?" Turner asked.

"He'd be impossible to work with, give short unhelpful answers to questions, mutter under his breath about what a treat they were missing. He was a superb organizer or Giles would have gotten rid of him long ago."

"Anybody talk about filing harassment suits against him?" Turner asked.

"Not that I know of. I think after a while the women laughed at him behind his back, but he was pretty persistent."

"You also didn't tell us about the fight between Giles and Ricken," Turner said.

"I heard Frank wanted to move onto green pastures. I didn't know they fought," Hank said.

They interviewed the other women in the room and Audrey again before they left. They confirmed, some of them reluctantly, that Ricken had been a sexist jerk.

"Why didn't anybody put a stop to it?" Turner asked.

Audrey said, "He was so inept at asking women for dates. He didn't take no for an answer, kept hinting about what we were missing. Thought he was quite the ladies' man. Don't know anybody who actually went out with him. He was a joke."

They didn't know about any fights recently and agreed with Hank that Ricken left because he had a better job offer.

Audrey said, "We told you all of this the other night when you interviewed us. Why are you asking again?"

"Because something about this organization doesn't make sense," Fenwick said. "Everybody talks as if everything were sweetness and light, and the only problem was a slightly over-sexed guy who nobody took seriously, and yet one guy's dead, one's missing, and one's beat-up. Ricken's parents said Giles and Ricken had a fight."

"None of us knew about it," Audrey said, then asked, "You don't think any of us killed him?"

"That's what we're trying to find out," Turner replied.

Mable Ashcroft, the chief of staff, entered. She saw the police and made a slow trek across the room to where they stood. She gave them a listless handshake and led them to an inner office. She put her elbows on the table and rested her chin in her cupped hands. "This is hell," she said.

121

"What is?" Turner asked.

"I haven't slept in twenty-four hours. I just spent three hours with Laura Giles. We used up three boxes of tissues. Gideon is dead. Ricken is god knows where. And Stimpson is hurt. A couple of days ago I was in an organization on its way up. Now it's all gone to crap. People keep calling asking for a thousand petty things. All the stupid groups we used to help want to know what's going to happen to them. You'd think they'd have the decency to wait until we buried the man."

"Why not close the office?" Turner asked.

"We debated it, but some of the people thought it would be better to try and keep busy. I don't know if it was the right thing to do. I'm not sure there is anything right left to do anywhere anymore. And I'm scared. There's a killer out there, or killers. Maybe stalking me."

Fenwick said, "We're working on that right now. We heard Ricken and Giles fought in the days before the alderman was murdered."

"Frank was a sexist fool, but a harmless one. He was always eager to have a demonstration, a march, set up a picket line. He thought those were actions that made a difference, and some times they could be a help to a cause, but he persisted and badgered. Gideon let him go, but I wouldn't call it a fight. Certainly there were no harsh words while I was around."

The cops tried a few questions about Stimpson.

Ashcroft said, "You went over this stuff yesterday. I've got nothing new to add. I'm more tired than I ever thought I could be in my entire life. I'm going home and take a pill and try and get some sleep."

"One last thing," Turner asked as he stood in the doorway. She gave him a weary look.

"Is there a health-food store around here that Giles used to go to?"

Ashcroft looked slightly startled for a moment then replied,

"He always went to the same one, I think. Place on the east side of Harper Court. Downstairs level."

Turner and Fenwick left with little to add to their meager store of knowledge. They stood on the paper littered sidewalk outside the campaign office/ward headquarters. Fenwick gazed at the kids playing on the swings in the playlot across the street. The temperature held in the low fifties, gray skies, but little chance of rain.

They drove to Harper Court. The owner of the health-food store, Henry Buchman, a man who looked to be in his early thirties with brush-cut hair, was effusive and friendly. "Sure, I knew the alderman," he said. "Came in all the time. Always friendly. Came in the first time ten years ago just after I opened the place. Usually bought juice. Always bought his weekly supply of vegetables on Monday mornings. Mixed and made his own special blends. Wanted me to try some once. Took a sip. Tasted awful."

"So he was in this Monday?" Turner asked.

"Sure. I remember he talked about helping us keep the court cleaned. I'm always here in the mornings, so I'd know."

Buchman told them Giles always brought five bottles of health-food juices, always different, and a selection of vegetables that varied every week.

In the car Fenwick said, "Not much help."

"At least it gives us a cut-off. Killer couldn't have put the poison in before Monday morning," Turner said.

"Killer could have broken in during the night," Fenwick said.

"Among the myriad of reports we've gotten is one from security at the university. No break-ins of any kind on campus for the forty-eight hours before the murder, and none in the English department for three years."

"Must your read all those reports?" Fenwick said.

"Habit," Turner said. "I'll try stopping."

"Who's got keys to the place?" Fenwick asked.

"Janitors and security. They've been interviewed. Nobody saw anything. All keys are accounted for."

"Only Carruthers would think it was an revenge-crazed janitor," Fenwick said.

Turner sighed. "At this moment I am dry of notions. Interviewing these politicians would make me jaded if I wasn't jaded already. Do any of them tell the truth?"

"I doubt it," Fenwick said. "The part that astounds me is that nobody knew Ricken and Giles fought. I don't buy that."

"Why protect Ricken?" Turner asked. "It doesn't make sense."

"This whole thing doesn't make sense," Fenwick said.

Turner picked up his notebook from the dashboard. He slowly perused the pages trying to find some link they hadn't tested several times.

He tapped Fenwick's shoulder and pointed to a name in the middle of a long paragraph. "We haven't talked to Lilac Ostergard, Laura Giles's best friend."

"I'm ready to bat my head against a brick wall," Fenwick said. "Where to?"

Turner consulted a list at the back of his regulation blue folder. He found the address and gave directions.

She lived on the east side of the ward. For those who thought of Chicago's south side as a large ghetto with the university stuck in the middle, Lilac Ostergard's neighborhood would have been a revelation. On street after street the homes were substantial with well-tended lawns. Fences protecting most of the homes testified to the high-crime areas around them.

S I X

The chimes sounded faintly through the solid oak door of Lilac Ostergard's home. She answered, stared at each of them from head to toe and pointed at them. "I remember you're police, but I don't recall your names. Come in."

She led them into a parlor done in metal furnishings. Two turn-of-the-century rocking chairs sat on either side of a marble-fronted fireplace. Wrought-iron antique candelabra stood on either side of silk-covered settees, which leaned against both walls. The three of them sat in griffin chairs grouped around a cast-iron-legged coffee table with a glass top.

Turner felt the stiffness of the chair on his back, yet didn't find the chair completely uncomfortable. A bay window was enshrouded by grey velvet curtains, which kept the light soft and muted. Lilac touched a button on the wall and a silver chandelier glowed to life, moving back a few of the shadows in the room. Sepia-toned portraits of children in eighteenth-century garb filled the walls.

Lilac wore a white woolen suit adorned with a sterling silver brooch. Turner explained about investigating the murder, then said, "We're hoping you can help us," he said. "We need to know about Laura and Gideon Giles. One thing we don't know is how involved Laura Giles was with her husband's campaigns."

Lilac leaned over and placed an elegant finger on Turner's arm. "Are you expecting me to implicate my best friend in the whole world?" Her voice murmured softly and seductively.

Turner said, "We just want what you can tell us. We're afraid she could be in danger as well as anyone connected with the Giles campaign."

She eyed each of them in turn. "I will be as truthful as I can." She leaned her head back, closed her eyes, and spoke without opening them. "Laura Giles and I grew up together on the near north side. We lived at Lake Point Towers. Sometimes I thought we were the only children in the whole building. We were wild, devils." She laughed, opened her eyes, and looked at them. "Laura Swift, that was her name then, was the most fun-loving person, prone to playing pranks, but her parents doted on her. She could do no wrong. In both homes the philosophy was the same, kids weren't supposed to get in the way of the career. So we played, mostly unsupervised. It was glorious."

She told them about going away to Stanford University, both on scholarships. Lilac and Laura'd continued their wild times in college. "They didn't have a party in that town that we didn't get begged to come to."

She sighed, "Then we both fell in love. With different men. We double-dated for a while, but I felt Laura drawing away. She got herself wrapped up with Giles. She came to her senses after a while. Realized no man was worth wasting that much time with. We pursued careers."

"So how'd she wind up married to Giles?" Turner asked.

"He offered her excitement, promised she could keep her own career. Claimed he didn't want kids. You can never trust a man on that. Eventually they all want a little junior to carry on after them." She tapped her fingernails on the edge of her chair. "In the past couple of years he put her under more and more pressure on the offspring issue. I told her he just wanted kids to have somebody on the platform with him. All those male politicians need to have their family around to prove their virility."

"How close were you to Laura?" Turner asked.

"Close enough to know the size of Gideon's penis, and I've never touched him or seen him naked. Laura and I talk every day on the phone. See each other for lunch at least once a week."

"Did Gideon Giles object to you being so close to his wife?" Fenwick asked.

"Didn't make any difference. She did as she pleased."

"They weren't a close couple," Turner said.

"Did they love each other, you mean?" Lilac said.

"I guess," Turner said.

"In a modern-marriage sort of way, yes. They did things together."

"Like what?"

"They loved to cook or go out dancing until all hours of the morning. When they started going out together, neither could cook very well and they enjoyed taking the same courses. Watched or taped every single one of those cooking shows on television. Plus Laura loved politics. She liked the glitz. I tried to break her of it. She claimed she knew it was all a sham, but she loved it anyway."

"We have it from several sources that Giles sold out to get himself elected," Fenwick said.

"I wouldn't know about that. I never got near the campaigns. Laura invited me all the time. I turned down every one."

"Did she ever talk about or express a concern about Gideon selling out?" Fenwick asked.

Lilac thought a minute. "No. He was pretty typical for a hard-driving white man. He'd thump his chest if he didn't get his way, but they all do that. Wanted to be more macho than thoughtful."

"He was involved in a lot of heart-tugging type of causes," Fenwick said.

"Old Gideon loved cheap sentiment. Loved what it could get him, and what he wanted to get was elected."

"Laura never mentioned some kind of deal that got him elected or helped him beat Mike McGee?"

"Nope."

They gave it up.

They called back to headquarters. Turner had two phone messages. One to call Mrs. Talucci, the other from Mary Ann Eliot.

They found a pay phone. Turner called Mrs. Talucci first. She rarely called him at work. If it was an emergency about one of the boys, she would have found a way to get hold of him without having to leave a message. As it was, he knew it had to be important.

"I've got you a meeting with somebody with real power in this city." She gave him an address on the west side of the city. She said, "It's for ten o'clock tonight and you have to go alone."

"Who is it?" Turner asked.

"You'll know when you meet him," Mrs. Talucci said.

"Why won't you tell me?" Turner asked.

Mrs. Talucci sighed. "Because I promised not to tell. I think it is best to accept the good fortune and leave it at that."

Turner knew he wouldn't get anything out of her she didn't want to tell. He checked the address. He didn't remember the neighborhood as the kind you took a casual stroll in at any time. "Is it safe to wander around there at that time of night?" he asked.

"I would never send you somewhere unsafe. A guard will meet you at the gate to the driveway. You have to go alone. He won't talk if you bring someone else. I trust him."

Turner knew he never should have doubted Mrs. Talucci. If she promised it would be safe, it would be. He dialed the number for Mary Ann Eliot.

"Nobody's talking to me," she said. "Everybody clams up when they hear what I want." She promised to keep trying.

Turner thanked her. He told her he had a possible lead into a political connection but didn't go into details. As he hung up, Fenwick called from the car, "Get in here. I've got some news."

Turner got back into the front seat of the car. Fenwick said, "While you were yapping with the women, I talked to Blessing at Area Ten."

"Did he find anything in the background checks?" Turner asked.

"We've got two strange connections so far, Blessing told me."

Which was two more than cops usually got from checking into backgrounds. "We've got clean records on the families, except for Giles's brother-in-law, Alex Hill."

"Don't remember anything special about the interview," Turner said. "My notes are at the station."

"They have him for assault on some ship while in the navy. Almost got court-martialed."

"Not much of a motivation for murdering his sister's husband," Turner said.

Fenwick said, "We also got the kid who was the secretary the day Giles got killed. He left the campaign organization about three months ago."

Turner gazed disgustedly at Fenwick.

"Kid tell you anything about knowing Giles before this?" Fenwick asked.

"Not a peep."

"Lying shit," Fenwick said.

"They all lie," Turner said.

"You must be really depressed about this case," Fenwick said.

Of all the detectives on the squad, Turner tried keeping a realistic perspective on the world. For all the cynicism concomitant with the job and the impossibility of solving every murder or stopping crime, he tried to hold onto a sense of proportion. Because one of the basic rules you learn as a detective is that everyone lies: every kind of criminal, half of major-crime witnesses, and an awful lot of cops. It's the detective that has to sift between lies and catch the glimmer of truth, if there is any to be found.

Murderers lie because they have to. Witnesses lie because they think they have to or to make themselves feel more important, maybe get themselves on a TV newscast. Many lie for the sheer joy of it, or to not give accurate information to the police on the general principle that it isn't a good idea to tell the police the truth.

"Goddamn kid is going to get his ass beaten," Turner said. "If he's got information, I'll get it out of him."

"Good," Fenwick said. Of the two of them usually it was he who had to be calmed down about taking a witness or suspect apart, although in all the years he'd known him, Turner had never seen Fenwick harm an innocent person.

As they drove, Turner told Fenwick about the interview Mrs. Talucci had set up.

"I don't like the idea of you going by yourself," Fenwick said. "I know you trust Mrs. Talucci, but does she really know these people well enough to believe they won't hurt you?"

"I have absolute faith in her," Turner said.

Fenwick grumbled about his going, until Turner reiterated,

"They won't talk to me if I bring somebody along. It'll work out."

"I hope so," Fenwick said, "but you should at least have a wire and backup a block away. I'll wait for you nearby."

"No wire. Let me think about back up." The partners trusted each other's judgement and Turner appreciated the concern.

They pulled off Lake Shore Drive at the Museum of Science and Industry. They took Fifty-ninth Street west to Woodlawn. A right on Woodlawn Avenue two blocks to the dorm.

The student at the downstairs desk stopped picking at a pimple long enough to glance at their identification and send them upstairs. Turner knocked on Burke's door. It swung open a moment later. Burke wore gauzy red running shorts, white socks, a sleeveless pullover sweatshirt that gathered tightly at the waist. He smiled at Turner.

Fenwick barged past them into the room.

Burke looked at Turner. "What's going on?"

They stood in the middle of the room facing each other.

Turner said, "You lied to me."

Burke's face turned crimson. Turner found the change attractive in an abstract way. He was pissed.

"About what?" Burke said.

"Cut out any kind of shit, kid," Fenwick said. "We don't like smart-ass kids who lie. We want some answers, and they better be what we want."

The kid looked to Turner, but the cop said, "Sit. Now."

Burke slowly sat in his chair. Turner wondered if the nineteen-year-old deliberately let his legs spread wide apart so his jock strap showed or if it was as unaffected as he pretended to be.

"Kid," Fenwick said, "you worked in Gideon Giles's campaign. You knew him before Tuesday when the murder occurred. You never mentioned it. We want to know why."

"I didn't lie," Burke said. At the furious look on Turner's

face he added, "Okay, I should have told you I knew him, but I didn't want to be involved in the murder. I was scared. If my parents found out, I'd be shipped back to Iowa on the first bus."

"But you called me back about your room," Turner said. "Why not just keep your mouth shut?"

Burke looked from Turner to Fenwick and back. He shifted in the chair so his legs were tight together.

Turner noted that the kid looked genuinely frightened. Turner knew he hadn't committed the murder. He was just a scared kid from off the farm who didn't know any better.

"I was afraid," Burke muttered.

"Of what?" Fenwick asked. "Of a real murderer? What the hell is it that you know?"

"Nothing," Burke's voice squeaked. "I swear, I don't know anything about the murder."

"But you know those people," Turner said, "you might be able to give us valuable information."

"I'm sorry," Burke said. "I didn't mean to screw up."

"Tell us what you know," Fenwick said. "We want everything you know about Giles and his organization."

"I just stuffed envelopes and answered phones," Burke said. He held out his hands, imploring them to believe him.

Turner felt sorry for the kid. He leaned against a poster of Jimmy Dean and said, "Okay, Burke, let's take it slow. You may know more than you think."

Burke told them about how six months ago he'd joined the campaign. A lot of the people on campus were signing up at the same time. It had been like a crusade, a fun thing to do, a way to meet people for someone new to the city. He'd gone two days a week up to the February election, with only time off for going home for Christmas and during finals.

"Did you know Frank Ricken?" Turner asked.

"Nice-looking blond in his mid thirties," Burke said. "He came around and tried to flirt with all the women who volun-

132

teered. Some of the younger ones got intimidated, but the older ones told him to get lost. He always came back for more. Kept trying to get dates. I never met anybody who could handle that much rejection."

"Did you know any of the women he asked?" Turner asked. "Anybody get mad enough to get revenge?"

"I didn't really get to know that many people that well. I think after a while all the women laughed at him, to his face. He never seemed to take it seriously."

Burke had only seen Giles three times and that at a distance, and never talked to him. "He gave us pep talks as a group during the campaign. He was really sincere. You could tell people liked him. He had a presence about him that you could trust, and he was for a lot of the causes I think are right."

"Like what?" Fenwick asked.

Burke's chin shot up. "Gay and lesbian rights was the main thing."

Turner said, "Did you ever see him and Ricken fight, argue, have angry words?"

"I don't think I ever saw the two of them together," Burke said. "The only problem I ever saw was with that Stimpson guy. I'm not sure people like him very much. He was always telling people what to do."

"He was only the media guy," Fenwick said. "Why would he be telling people what to do?"

Burke shrugged. "I don't know. He just did."

"Why didn't people like it?" Turner asked.

"I mean," Burke said, "that he was unnecessarily abrupt. If there was a nice way to say something and a nasty way, he always seemed to pick the nasty way."

"Anybody specific he picked on?" Fenwick asked.

"Not really." Burke thought a minute. "I did see him and Ricken arguing a couple times. I remember someone in our group saying that if Ricken had his way maybe we'd get something done."

"What wasn't getting done?" Turner asked.

"Lots of the volunteers wanted to get involved in the causes. I wanted to go to Springfield and lobby for gay rights."

"That's hardly something that would be on an alderman's agenda. What could he hope to accomplish by trying to intervene with the state legislature?" Turner asked.

"It was in his gay-rights platform statement," Burke said. "That we would take busloads of people down to lobby in the state capital."

"They ever go?" Turner asked.

"No. Something else always came up. I mentioned it to Ricken one time and he told me to try and stick with the campaign. That if Giles didn't get it accomplished, no other politician would. That none of the others cared enough or dared to take on tough causes."

"Other politicians in this state have been fighting for gay rights for years," Turner said.

"They don't much in my state. I didn't know about Illinois. At least Giles made the promise."

"Why'd you quit?" Turner asked.

"I got bored," Burke said. "I suppose I could have stuck it out, but the campaign was over, and they didn't really seem to want us around."

"Who didn't want you around?" Turner asked.

"Stimpson, Ashcroft. We'd show up and want to work on gay rights, but they told us to go home and wait for them to call us. I talked to a few other people, and they said the same thing happened to all the other causes, except for a few of Giles's pet ones."

"Which ones were those?" Turner asked.

Burke frowned. "I'm not sure I remember. Is it important?"

"We won't know until you tell us," Fenwick said.

"I guess, the Save the Lakefront people seemed pretty happy, maybe the Friends of the Zoo, I think all the animal-rights activists were pretty pleased. I really don't know."

"A rebellion of zoo keepers," Fenwick grumbled.

Burke stared at him.

They asked more questions, but got no further answers that got them closer to solving the murder.

Fenwick walked out the door of the room first. Burke tapped Turner on the shoulder. The cop turned back.

"I'm sorry," Burke said. The teenager looked handsome and contrite. He was slender, but muscular, his blond hair winsomely falling into his eyes. He asked, "Could I meet you for a cup of coffee sometime?"

Turner gazed into the youthful eyes. "For what?" he asked.

"I'd like to talk to you, about—" Burke hung his head. "I'd just like to talk," he mumbled.

Turner said he'd get back to Burke about a time, but made no promises. The murder investigation would keep him too busy for days.

"What'd he want?" Fenwick asked as they strode past the Robie House back to the car.

"He wants to get together for coffee."

Fenwick stopped and said, "He's got a crush on you."

Turner shrugged. "Maybe."

"I am an insensitive white heterosexual male, and even I noticed the looks he snuck at you," Fenwick said. "I wasn't going to say anything because I figured you weren't interested."

"I'm not interested. I don't date kids. I like guys my age. Ben is more than enough, besides which I love him."

"By meeting with the kid, you'd be encouraging him," Fenwick said.

"I didn't encourage him. He's a suspect in a murder case. If he wants to talk, I'll talk. If he wants to have sex, he'll have to find someone his own age."

In the car Fenwick said, "Let's try back at the Fifth Ward office. Some of those idiots have to have realized something was wrong. We need to lean harder on them."

Turner agreed, but when they got to the ward office, it was closed. They returned to Area Ten headquarters.

Outside they saw two separate Minicam trucks from local television stations. Bright lights shone on reporters taping for the late news. One of the reporters recognized Turner and Fenwick and came running over. Her rush to them spurred the interest of the other crew. In seconds lights, microphones, and inquisitive reporters blocked their way into the station. Turner recognized a few of the regulars on the crews by sight. Often given the high-profile murder cases to solve, he had gotten to know some of them. The reporters shied away from Fenwick. He was known never to give information, and to become nasty if pushed. Turner never told them anything he shouldn't, but he was friendly with them, and they liked to put him on the news because of his good looks.

A needle-nosed, blond reporter asked him if they had any leads. Turner gave her a smile and a bland quote. She looked frustrated, but before the pack could move in for more, Turner and Fenwick edged into the building.

Inside they met with the case sergeant, the commander, the other detectives on the squad, and with the people doing background checks. They told the commander about the reporters.

He said, "They've been hanging around all day. One of those idiots has made it a crusade. They're already talking about a 'Chicago-style cover-up.' He claims that somehow we're going to suppress the identity of one of the most notorious killers in this city in years. If I'd known you were coming back, I'd have found something to keep them busy. You don't need this kind of nonsense, although I've got to tell you, the pressure is enormous. We've got national publicity coming down on us. 'Sixty Minutes' plus one other national television news magazines called. Giles wasn't really big time nationally, but that media consultant Stimpson had an enormous national reputation. They want reports, information, and access, especially to you guys."

"Double fuck," Fenwick said.

"I'll keep them away from you as best I can, but this is bigger than anything I've handled as long as I've been here." The commander shook his head. "Any progress?"

They told him all they'd done.

He gave them a few suggestions, all of which they'd already tried, but wise in the ways of the hierarchy, they didn't tell him that, and then Turner and Fenwick got to their desks.

They started the reams of paperwork. They began filing and cross-referencing tons of interviews and mounds of data. They paused in that work for half an hour to visit Blessing. They spent most of that time poring over an enormous diagram Blessing had prepared of all the people in the Ricken, Stimpson, and Giles families, anyone connected to them politically, and the prominent people in the city who backed Giles or whom he had supported.

As they stared at the diagram, Blessing said, "I got more charts coming on any organizations Giles championed. They'll be cross-referenced with all these. Eventually you'll be able to tell who knew who and what their relationship was in one glance." They took one fourth floor wall and tacked the four-by-six-foot sheet up. Turner and Fenwick started at opposite ends and studied it carefully.

They met in the middle and Fenwick said, "Double and triple fuck. What the shit are we supposed to get out of this?"

"The name of the killer. Or maybe the secret to winning the lottery," Turner said.

On another wall Blessing was taping up copies of all the campaign literature, using two copies if one was printed on both sides.

"Why put all that up?" Fenwick asked him.

"I want everything organized," Blessing said. "I sent over

for extra copies of things you only had one of. Gives me something to do when all the letters on the computer screen begin to blur."

"Don't waste too much time on it," Turner said. He glanced at the first row that Blessing had already attached. He saw lots of glossy pictures with tons of smiling people in them. He shrugged, checked the time. "I got to go meet my source."

"What about backup?" Fenwick asked.

"If it's fatal, whether you're here or a block away, I'd be dead before you could get to me. Forget it."

"Be careful," Fenwick warned. "Keep your radio handy, and your gun close by. Call as soon as you're done. I'll be here."

Turner took Wells Street north, turned left onto the beginning of the Eisenhower Expressway, drove under the Main Post Office, and headed west.

He got off the Expressway at Sacramento Avenue. He drove four blocks south to Polk Street and turned west. A few blocks west and he stopped outside an anomaly. The quiet street lined with trees had mostly three flats, gray stones, or frame houses. In the middle of the block three bungalows stood side by side, out of place, well lit, neatly kept, and fenced in. In this poor neighborhood with boarded-up buildings and vacant lots well in evidence, this was more than an oddity.

Turner parked in the driveway that led to an opening in the fence. He didn't see anyone. He surveyed his surroundings carefully. This wasn't a neighborhood he'd choose to be caught in unprepared. He checked his gun and radio, then left the car.

As soon as his feet touched the pavement, bright lights shone on him, the porch light of the house flicked on, and three snarling Doberman pinschers raced around the corner of the center house. A six-foot-six, well-over 250-pound man descended the steps and lumbered toward him.

Turner felt the cool spring breeze touch the back of his

neck. He walked to the gate. The man said nothing to Turner. He quieted the dogs, unlatched the gate, and motioned Turner to enter.

"I'm here to talk to . . ."

The man's rough voice interrupted, "We know why you're here, and you're expected."

Turner was curious. "How do you know I'm the right guy?"

"If you were the wrong guy, you wouldn't get out of here alive."

"Oh," Turner said.

They crossed the clipped lawn. Turner observed well-tended hedges and in the bright lights still shining from when they turned to focus on him, he saw well-preserved homes, the paint recent, the dark-maroon bricks cleaned and scrubbed.

The man led Turner quickly through the house and to the basement stairs. Turner's brief view showed him a living room filled with furniture enshrouded in plastic coverings.

At the top of the stairs the bulky factotum faced Turner, thumped a beefy finger into the cop's chest, and said, "You shouldn't be here. If it was up to me, you'd never leave."

Before Turner could respond, the man turned his back and began stomping down the steps. Downstairs Turner walked into a comfortable room. Dark wood paneling, a gold deep-pile rug, brass lamps on teak end tables, cloth armchairs, a rocking chair, a seven-foot sofa, and a white ceiling. Pictures of sporting scenes covered one of the walls. The others were bare.

On the sofa sat a tiny shriveled-up old man. Turner had never seen so many wrinkles on a human being. The man's cheeks sagged almost to bloodhound length.

"Forgive me for not rising," he said. Turner could barely hear the voice.

"Want me to take his gun, boss?" Turner's escort said.

The man waved him away, then smiled at Turner. The cop saw two gray teeth and pink gums and hoped the guy didn't make a habit of smiling at him.

"And I'm sure he doesn't have a wire," the old man said. "You may leave us." The hulk left.

Turner had recognized the man instantly. Even in his old age, the face was unmistakable, this was Giovanni Parelli, ex-alderman, reputed mob boss, and in his day, one of the most-feared men in the city.

"Mrs. Talucci loves you," the aged voice said. "Says you have two nice boys. That you're a good father. I like that."

Turner waited.

Parelli couldn't have weighed more than a hundred pounds. He wore a long-sleeved white shirt buttoned to the collar, but no tie. A gold wedding ring gleamed on one of his withered and age-spotted hands.

"She wants me to help you." He chuckled and smiled again. "Rose Talucci." The voice became softer and more distant. "We grew up together. I introduced her to her husband. Good man. But it was a mistake. I thought I had a chance for her hand myself, but after they met, she only had eyes for Frank." He patted one hand with the other. "I've known Rose since I was three years old. Pulled her pigtails when I was five." He laughed. "She didn't run to her mother. She slapped me so hard, my ears rang for a week. I've never been able to refuse a request of hers."

"She's a good friend," Turner said.

Parelli said, "A great lady. I can refuse her nothing. My wife died in an accident. Rose was a second mother to my five children. She is a saint. She says you don't understand several things about this murder. I'll do what I can to help you, young man." He smiled again.

"I don't understand the politics of the Fifth Ward in connection with the killing," Turner said.

"I knew Vito Marzullo, Jake Avery, all the old-time politicians, now fewer and fewer people remember them, but I still have connections, and the old wheel spins around and comes up the same."

Turner said, "I don't understand."

"Dirty tricks," Turner said. "Everybody knows Nixon didn't invent them. We've had masters at the art of making the other guy look bad since the first settlers did the trick on the Indians when this was all still prairie."

"I don't get . . ." Turner began.

Parelli waved his hand at him. "You need to be silent and listen."

Turner shut up.

"Do you remember the Red Squads?" Parelli asked.

Turner nodded. Back in the thirties and forties the Chicago police department began spying on suspect, mostly left-wing, groups. This accelerated during the McCarthy years. In the sixties they infiltrated the antiwar movement. They were accused of sending "agent provocateurs" into the organizations. A suit was filed to make the police stop the spying and any other activities. After many years a judge ruled against the police. Even in the nineties the consent decree still held that said they weren't supposed to do such things.

"That kind of infiltration wasn't effective enough. Plus they got caught. We found another way. Most of the people in the groups who wanted change in this city were made up of wild-eyed fools who couldn't have run a meeting much less made a success out of a cause, but they mastered the art of catching the press's eye and the powers that are in this city don't like fighting their battles in the full glare of the media."

The six-foot-six man appeared with a glass of chalky liquid. Parelli asked if Turner would like something. The cop said no thanks. The old man took several gulps and left about half the liquid unconsumed. "Doesn't even taste bad anymore," he said.

"I hope you aren't ill," Turner said.

141

"My internal organs have been trying to shut down for decades. I'm surprised I'm still alive." He gave several soft chuckles. The guard/servant left.

"So we had to diffuse these people. The chaos in the groups was obvious. We needed to feed that. We'd get people into their organizations who were masters of bringing up divisive issues. If a group was mostly white, we'd embroil them in issues of lack of race representation, playing on the guilt of white people. No mind that black people didn't want to be part of their organizations or hadn't even heard of them. Same tactic with women's equality. Our people were always the biggest supporters of equal representation of men and women: equal co-chairs, vice co-chairs, shared treasurer, and secretary duties. One great way was to fight over who to accept funding from. Was it pure to take money from suspect sources." He chuckled for a minute. "That was my particular favorite. The mischief we could make would be endless. We'd get the groups so embroiled in side issues that had nothing to do with their basic cause, they'd never get anything done. The brightest and most eager people would give up. Our opposition crippled, we'd have many fewer problems."

Turner was enough of a realist to know that politics in Chicago had never been like an afternoon tea with the queen of England, but Parelli's cynicism bothered him. He swallowed a comment but wasn't able to mask his disapproval completely.

Parelli caught the look and said, "What you'd really like to say is that you're shocked and appalled." The old grey eyes searched his. "Admit it, young man. You think this is a horrible way for democracy to work."

"I'm just trying to solve a murder. If I got involved in every political or emotional side issue, I'd never get anywhere."

"A sensible answer."

"But," Turner began and the old man chuckled. Turner continued, "You couldn't be sure of being effective with every group, and it would take enormous resources," Turner said.

Parelli mused for several minutes then said, "We could be

fairly sure, because we co-opted all the other do-gooders. The resources part was easy. Wise political pundits have declared the Chicago machine dead for many years." The crinkled old face gave another awful grin. "Those of us in the know, keep our mouths shut. We've got a lot of the old guard and a few new ones. We've got plenty of people to call on. For all the upheaval of the past few years, remember the person who's won the Democratic primary has won the mayor's office for over fifty years."

"But Giles was against the party and he supported all the reform causes," Turner said. "He must have been a huge threat to the organization. Who would be powerful enough or have sufficient money to influence a ward election? We can't find any evidence of any of the groups Giles backed or who supported him being rich or powerful or connected enough to cause him to win. Even Mike McGee may have been a maverick, but he still had enough sense to not go too far. He was still the one passing out the jobs and favors."

"Old Mike knew what was best." Parelli took a few more sips of the chalky liquid, pulled out a starched white hanky and dabbed at the corners of his mouth. He said, "The reason you can't figure out who the powerful and rich people are who supported Giles is, you're looking in the wrong place. You haven't understood what I've been trying to tell you. You're assuming the Democratic party would be against him. That's your mistake. First of all no individual group has enough clout to overthrow a sitting alderman, not without a major change in the ward's racial or ethnic population, or barring a major snowstorm."

This last reference was to the mayoral election of 1979 when then-Mayor Bilandic told the citizens of the city that their streets were clear of snow. It was a tough winter with record snow and the good citizens could look out their windows to their lawns, cars, and streets buried in drifts of white. The blunder cost him the election.

"So the alderman in the Fifth Ward retired. We needed a base, a front that everyone would assume was legitimately liberal. What better than the Fifth Ward? We saw our chance. It was one of the great races. We ran three candidates. The one from the regular machine, who got rewarded with a judgeship. A real reformer who was a fool, and our man Giles."

"But you didn't get rid of McGee," Turner said.

"Wasn't necessary at first, but eventually we had to dump old Mike. We were afraid he might catch on. For an Irishman he was pretty smart. That was also a payback among the Irish politicians themselves. They've hated him for years."

"So all that talk from Gideon Giles was hypocritical rhetoric."

"Yes. He was our bought and paid stooge from the beginning."

"Does the mayor know this?"

"Politics in this city is Byzantine, as you know. Would he have specifically ordered something like this? No. Do members of his inner circle know the truth? Of course."

"Could other people have figured this out? Maybe somebody caught on or caught Giles and was threatening to expose the whole thing?"

Parelli thought a moment then said, "I haven't heard anything. Look at how long it's been going on and none of the papers have breathed a word, and my guess is they don't know anything. The easy story was to go interview Gideon Giles. Why break your neck trying to prove something as hard to track down as a conspiracy to do good?" He chuckled.

Turner said, "I wish I found this harder to believe."

Parelli said, "When we were young, we wanted power. Then we wanted to keep it. These people want power. Someday they'll probably have it, but they're going to have to become a whole lot tougher and smarter." He laughed.

Turner said, "What about people being afraid of the whole

scheme being known. Wouldn't that make someone frightened?"

"First of all I would know if people were frightened of the scheme coming out. No one in any organization has threatened to expose us. I have heard nothing. What I'm telling you is that no politician had any reason to get rid of Gideon Giles, certainly no one in City Hall. Second, if you're an outsider, why kill Giles and beat up the others? If you found out they were doing something criminal, you'd run to the press. You wouldn't need to murder anybody."

"Disillusionment. You've revered these people as leaders of a cause. In your frustration you murder them."

Parelli reached over and patted Turner's knee. "Young man, if you really believe that, you'd better turn in your badge. Radical do-gooders don't do murder."

Turner flushed slightly. He wasn't ready to abandon his idea about insiders at City Hall being worried about the scheme being revealed. He asked, "Who, besides Giles, among his people, knew he was backed by the party?"

"I believe it was just him. If someone in Giles's organization found out, and they confronted him, wouldn't Giles be more likely to try and do something to him, rather than someone do something to Giles?"

"If a true believer thought their cause had been betrayed, they might try anything. You're probably right, no one would really buy a conspiracy by liberal reformers, but the person who was in the best position to blow the thing out of the water is dead, and of the two people in the campaign most likely to know, one's been beaten and won't tell us anything. The other is missing. Supposedly they were closest to him."

Turner sat silently for several minutes and thought. The old man kept quiet. Turner moved to the edge of his chair. "What if it was Giles himself who was going to blow the whistle? What if he'd decided to end the sham? It would ruin his career, but he could drag down a lot of politicians. Maybe he had an attack of conscience. If he was going to turn on his backers, those in danger might be willing to do something vicious to stop him."

Parelli shut his eyes and was silent for a long time. Turner thought he might have fallen asleep. When the old eyes snapped open, they looked pained. "You bring up an intriguing possibility. Young man, I have heard of no such problem or conspiracy. Gideon Giles never struck me as a man with any kind of conscience. I've never met a man more driven by ambition." He cleared his throat, pulled out his handkerchief, and spit into it. Parelli said, "I may be old, but I still hear everything that is to be heard among the powers in the city. I will check your theory. It will take some time."

Turner thanked him and prepared to leave.

Parelli waved him to remain seated. "There is something you must know. If you are even remotely correct, that shot fired at you could have been a warning. Rose was quite angry about that. I don't control such things. I cannot guarantee your safety, but I will do what I can for her sake to protect you. The situation is volatile. People might want to prevent what you might uncover from coming out. Frankly that shot is the main thing that leads me to think there might be something behind your idea. When Rose told me about the shooting, I assumed it was random violence, but I checked. I was not told it was to warn you off. I will talk to people again. I am not so old that they can lie to me with impunity. I advise you to be careful. If I have been lied to, then I have a problem, but you need to be extremely wary. They may or may not be capable of murder to prevent a conspiracy coming to the light of day, but they would be happy to frighten you from telling the truth. Gideon may not have been murdered to shut him up, but people could want to be sure you aren't a loose cannon."

"I'm a cop, Mr. Parelli. I'm going to do my job. I have to solve this murder, just like any other. I won't hold back."

146

Parelli smiled at him. "Just be careful. Take it as a well-meant warning. I will do what I can for you."

The bodyguard met him at the top of the stairs.

"I can see myself out," Turner said.

The man mumbled and walked out to the gate with him. The man watched Turner unlock his car. As the cop opened the door the guy said, "If you ever come back here, you will be sorry. People can disappear in this city."

Turner stared back for a moment but said nothing. He used his radio to call Area Ten. He left a message to tell Fenwick to go home and they'd talk in the morning. Nothing could be done tonight. Parelli would never tell him who his sources were, much less let him interview them. Turner wasn't ready for taking on the most powerful politicians in the city. Supposedly the police department was much less political than it was before O. W. Wilson cleaned it up back in the early sixties, but one cop didn't have much chance against the power that could be mustered against him. If the politicians were behind this, he could be in deep trouble.

He eased his car into his driveway. It was nearly eleven-thirty, and the lights were out in Mrs. Talucci's house. A lamp burned in his living room. Paul could see Ben Vargas reading a magazine.

Ben stood up as Paul walked in. Ben was one of the few people Paul was aware of who still wore pajamas, at least the bottoms. Ben never wore the tops. Paul hugged the hirsute chest and gave him a kiss. "What are you doing here?" he whispered.

"You're not glad to see me?" Ben asked.

"Delighted, but surprised."

"I had to stop at Mrs. Talucci's tonight. One of her daughters had some trouble with a car, and I came over. You'd given Brian permission to stay over at a friend's house to study. Mrs. Talucci claimed a family emergency had come up and she had to go out, so she asked if I could look after Jeff, and wait for you to come home. I think she may have been fibbing. She uses any excuse to get me to stay over here, especially to be with the kids."

"She's an old matchmaker," Paul said. "She won't be happy until we officially get married."

"I look silly in a white veil," Ben said.

"But you look very sexy in a tux," Paul said. They held each other and kissed. "Let's go to bed," Ben murmured.

Paul checked on the peacefully sleeping Jeff, then joined Ben. The pajama bottoms didn't stay on long.

SEVEN

The next morning Paul asked Jeff about his homework.

"Ben helped me," Jeff said. "He knows a lot of math."

Ben, taking Brian's place at cooking breakfast, added, "He just wanted to get his homework done so he could beat me at his Nintendo games."

Jeff said, "He's better than you are, Dad. He almost beat me once."

Paul congratulated his younger son on his wizardry at electronic games as the front door banged open and Brian bounced into the room. He said breezy hello's to everybody, grabbed some toast and milk, and started wolfing them down.

"How do you manage to be so energetic in the morning?" Ben asked.

"Big plans today. People to see. Baseball practice." He

paused between gulps of milk. He looked at his dad. "Unless you're going to work and need help with Jeff."

Paul hated to interfere with Brian's schedule on short notice. His older son gave up huge amounts of his time to take care of his brother, and this was a sacrifice because Brian was a popular athlete with a busy social life. He knew Brian would do it, but one of Paul's unwritten rules was to make sure both boys had their lives impeded as little as possible because of the help Jeff needed. Also, it was Paul's problem that he had to go into work, not Brian's.

"I'll have to check with Mrs. Talucci. Somebody will have to watch Jeff."

"Jeff can come to the shop if he wants," Ben offered.

"He'd be in the way."

"No I wouldn't, Dad. It would be cool. If Myra is there, she might let me help. She did last time."

"You shouldn't bother people at the shop," Paul said.

"It wasn't a bother," Ben said. "He and Myra like each other."

"She told me she was a lesbian, Dad. That's just like you and Ben, only with women."

Paul patted his son's head. "At least you learned something."

"So can I go, Dad, please?"

"I'll have to check with Mrs. Talucci. That way if you change your mind or get tired, you'll have a place to go."

"How's the case going, Dad?" Brian asked.

Paul shook his head. "I'll be at work all day and probably half the night. I'm afraid I won't be able to make Jeff's game."

Jeff had recently joined a wheelchair basketball league. He wasn't very good yet, but the coach made sure all the kids on the team played for at least four or five minutes. Paul had been to all of the games so far and even stopped in at some of the practices. "I'll give it my best shot."

"I can pick up Jeff at Ben's and drive him to the game," Brian said.

Paul told Brian he could use the van since he'd be taking Jeff. Paul would use Brian's car for transportation.

"Pick you up at five, squirt." Brian tossled his brother's hair. Seconds later they heard the thud of his feet on the stairs up to his room.

Paul checked with Mrs. Talucci. If Jeff got bored or in the way, she would take care of him. Mrs. Talucci smiled when Paul said Ben would take Jeff to work with him. Paul also thanked Mrs. Talucci for getting him in to talk to Parelli.

"How could you be involved with such a notorious guy?" Paul asked.

"Notorious, ha! As far as I'm concerned he's still running from me as I chased him down Taylor Street eighty years ago. Tried to steal a kiss in the park. Needs a good slap upside the head. Married Maria Borasini. She knew how to keep him in line. He did his political nonsense and kept out of her way, but she died." Mrs. Talucci paused. "I did help him with the children. Maria was my best friend when we were growing up."

"Did he really introduce you to Frank?" Paul asked.

"Ah, yes. But I'll save that story for sometime when I'm old and have nothing else to talk about." As he began to leave she added, "Be careful with Giovanni Parelli. I trust him only so far. I raised his children, but still, I know he's a crook. He will look out for himself. Be careful."

Turner thanked her for the warning and left.

Paul called Ian before he left for Area Ten. It was nine-thirty on a Saturday morning, earlier than he would normally call his friend. Ian swore angrily until he realized it was Turner, then he just grumbled and complained. Turner said he would pick him up in fifteen minutes. Ian squawked protests, but Turner told him he wanted to talk about political conspiracies and Giovanni Parelli.

"Parelli doesn't exist. He's a figment of the conspiracy theorists," Ian said.

"I met him last night," Turner said. He hung up on Ian's exclamations of disbelief.

Turner picked the reporter up at Clark and Diversey and drove to the Breakfast Club on Hubbard Street. Ian wore a longsleeve sweatshirt that said, NO ONE KNOWS I'M A SHIT, light blue jeans, and gym shoes with no socks. He kept his slouch fedora pulled well over his eyes.

"Disturbing my Saturday-morning beauty sleep is a serious crime," Ian said.

"No one knows better than I how much beauty sleep you really need," Turner said.

"You are forgiven for that crack only because you claim you met Giovanni Parelli."

"Not a claim," Turner said. "I did."

"Any reporter in the city would give his left nut for an interview with the guy," Ian said.

"All the reporters in the city are male?" Turner asked.

"The women would give their left tit. How the hell did you manage to get close to him."

"Mrs. Talucci," Turner said.

"Old Rose is a gangster! I always wondered what her connection was. She's a sly old devil."

"She always liked you," Turner said.

"She's also perceptive and wise. Now what the hell is going on?"

Turner told Ian what had happened. Turner knew that he could trust his friend to keep a confidence, even though Ian was a reporter. Plus he needed information.

After Turner finished, Ian said, "You could talk to Mary Ann Eliot again."

"I'm not sure I want to trust any politician in this city. She's probably okay, but I'd rather not, at the moment. And think about it. None of her leads has given us much of anything. If it wasn't for Rose, I wouldn't be this far."

1 5 2

They arrived at the restaurant, which was in a converted home two blocks east of Ashland Avenue on Hubbard Street, just a block or so from the Northwestern railroad tracks. They were lucky, it wasn't crowded and they were seated immediately.

After they ordered, Ian said, "You know this whole conspiracy to undermine the reformers that Parelli outlined has a certain sublime elegance, but Giles couldn't have been the only one in the group who knew about it. He had to have trained the people who went to these groups to undermine them. They would be able to turn on him. How could he trust people who just showed up as volunteers?"

"The volunteers," Turner said, "could go to as many different groups they wanted to. The key was that one person from the Democratic organization went to the various group meetings. That person would be trained from downtown. No need to trust amateurs who walked in off the street."

"The conspirators weren't volunteers?" Ian asked.

"Nope. They showed up as if they were volunteers. No one else in Giles's organization had to know," Turner said. "You believe what Parelli told me?"

"Hell of question to ask me. I wasn't there."

"Could it be true? You know these liberal reform organizations better than I do. Could somebody have been undermining them all these years?"

"I'm not sure," Ian said.

"It was easy to believe last night," Turner said. "It was spooky being in the house. I almost expected corpses to stick out of the woodwork. That it looked so ordinary made it even creepier."

"Everybody lies," Ian mused, "so what part of it would Parelli have been lying about."

As a former cop, he too had suspicions about what people told him. They talked over all the ramifications of what Parelli had said as they finished their meal and had coffee and blueberry scones for dessert. Ian swallowed a last bite, brushed his fingers off, and said, "I think you're in danger. I think Giles had people in most organizations. And I think the whole thing is totally screwed up. Can't see how you're going to find the murderer. What do you want me to do to help?"

"Your connections in some of the do-good organizations. See if you can't talk to a few of them. Find the kind of person Parelli described. An obstructionist. I'd like to talk to at least one of them."

"I know the heads of lots of these groups," Ian said. "I'll find out what I can."

"See what you can uncover, but be careful. I don't want you in danger."

Ian pushed his hat back and revealed dark-red hair. Turner knew he only took the slouch fedora off to go to bed. Ian said, "I could take care of myself even before I was a cop."

Turner drove to Area Ten headquarters. It was just eleven. Fenwick drove up while Turner was walking from the parking lot to the door. He waited for his friend, and they strode in together. They checked with the commander and the case sergeant to see if any new leads had come up before they'd gotten in. Nothing had.

Turner gave Fenwick all the details about his meeting with Parelli. They discussed it and agreed they'd have to wait to hear from the old man. They would try to develop their own leads with the politicians only if the old man didn't come through or if he delayed and they thought he was playing games.

After working an hour they got a call from John Chester. The bar owner told them he hadn't been able to find out anything.

For two more hours they plowed through paperwork. Over a cup of coffee and a doughnut, their first break all afternoon, Fenwick said, "Okay this political bullshit might lead somewhere, but what about these University people. I've been going through all the interviews with the minor office workers, peripheral people, and I get a sense that all was not good between Giles and the rest of the faculty."

"When you and I talked to them, they seemed to be talking about only the usual petty jealousies any faculty would have."

"Being around those academic shits probably warped your mind. I'm suspicious, and I'm not convinced. And I don't like those academic shits. I want to look at them. I need to see their faces, watch them squirm. These notes don't do shit."

"Who's going to be around on a Saturday?" Turner asked.

Fenwick licked the remnants of several doughnuts off his fingers and plunged through his pile of paperwork. He emerged with a list of addresses along with a cover letter, glanced at it, and said, "Says here that lots of them hang around the Quadrangle Club, plus lots of these folks live in Hyde Park. Let's go visiting."

In the car, Turner looked through the list of names. "Giles's regular secretary at the University is supposed to be back from vacation today." He found her address. "Let's try her first."

"Which one was she?"

"Gwendolen Harleth." Turner hunted through a pile of forms, found the one he wanted. "Blessing checked her out. She was legitimately on vacation. Been planned for months."

"Maybe the killer knew that," Fenwick offered.

"Maybe," Turner said. "She should have lots of background on all the university people." He gave Fenwick the address on East Madison Park.

Madison Park lies between Dorchester and Woodlawn Avenues in Hyde Park between Fifty-first and Fiftieth streets. On each end of the three-block stretch are iron fences and signs that say PRIVATE. It is one of 123 private streets listed in the Chicago street guide. Residents pay for all the upkeep. The one-way road winds through an urban sanctuary of trees, shrubbery, and grass. The street is lined with homes and luxury apartment buildings.

They pulled up in front of what was perhaps the most

modest of the homes. A dark-blue Dodge van sat in the drive-way. The sliding doors were open on the sides. Bags of grocer-ies waited to be lugged into the house. A woman emerged from inside and strode down the driveway to them. She smiled at the cops uncertainly. They showed her their identification.

She was five-foot-two, wearing a tan warm-up suit with a hooded sweatshirt. Her graying hair lay flat against the sides of her head. Turner guessed her to be in her late fifties.

"I heard while I was on vacation," she said. "One of the secretaries had my itinerary."

"We need to ask you some questions," Turner said.

She nodded. The cops each grabbed a sack of groceries and carried them in for her. They talked in the kitchen while she put away groceries. A sun room that faced west led directly off the kitchen. Bright light streamed through all the windows and lit up a jungle of green plants. Turner and Fenwick sat at the kitchen table. As she stored her supplies, Turner noted she did so carefully, placing each item just so.

Turner asked, "How long were you Gideon Giles's secre-tary?"

"Since I started at the university, eight years ago."

"Tell us about him," Turner said.

She paused with the refrigerator door open and looked at them. Turner saw tears in her eyes. "He was a good boss, according to his lights. I had to set him straight a few times. I'll never forget the first day when I told him I wouldn't make or fetch his coffee. His mouth gaped open in the most amusing way."

"You must have been pretty confident to say something like that the first day," Fenwick said.

"No," she said. "I just know what I will or won't do, and I've been around the University long enough to know what was tolerated. He took it well. We had a good relationship. He tried to get me to do some of his political work, but I refused. Told him I was his secretary at the University, and I would do

156

anything for him I could, but I wouldn't get involved in his politics."

"You didn't know any of the politicians?" Fenwick asked.

She folded the paper bags and placed them in a rack next to the refrigerator. She sat with them at the table. She said, "I recognized some of the names he had appointments with, and some of the people who came in looked familiar from pictures in the newspapers, but it wasn't my business and wasn't my job, so I didn't pay much attention."

"I looked in his appointment book," Turner said. "He had only one meeting Monday and another Tuesday."

"That sounds right. I kept his schedule for him. He could have had more political things to do, but if he did, someone from the campaign would call, but I don't remember anything else. What was on the calendar should have been it."

"How did he get along with other people in the University?" Turner asked.

She sighed. "How much do you know about University people?" she asked.

They shrugged. Turner said, "Not much."

Harleth explained that her husband had been a professor at the university. She hadn't had a degree and didn't want to get one, but they were in love and had gotten married. The other professors' wives, especially the ones with degrees, sneered and looked down on her. "It's a catty competitive world among the professors and among their husbands or wives," she said. But she and her husband had been secure in their love. He'd died ten years ago. She'd worked as a secretary for many years for a law firm in the Loop, but after her husband's death, she had been devastated. She hadn't worked for a year after. They'd invested wisely and saved so she didn't have to work, but she wanted a few luxuries, and she wanted to keep busy. She'd seen an opening at the university, applied, and gotten it.

"University people tend to live in a closed society," she said. "Lots of ambition and infighting. You listen closely to a lot of their conversations, it's nothing but put-downs of each other. Sometimes somebody says something genuinely funny, but usually it's hurtful stuff."

"Like what?" Turner said.

"When my husband was alive, I'd go to parties with him. Most of the time I'd sit quietly and listen. It was incredible. They'd snipe at each other about who got reviewed and who didn't and what the reviews said. They'd maneuver to get appointed to committees or fight about who was closer to the chairman of the department, who was or wasn't going to get tenure. Men, women, they were all vicious about it. When I came to work it was the same thing."

"How did Giles fit into that?" Fenwick asked.

She told them she'd known Giles slightly while her husband was alive. "He seemed pretty much like the rest, until this political business started."

"What happened then?" Turner asked.

"It got much worse. A group of us faculty wives would get together once a week for lunch. We'd gossip about what was going on. Then when I became a secretary, a bunch of us ate lunch every day. We used to laugh about how pompous and absurd they were, but the professors took it all very seriously. When Giles started his political career, a lot of the other professors didn't like it that he got all that publicity in the press. Some of them complained that it brought down the dignity of the institution to have someone connected to the University involved in the gutter politics of the city. I think some of them were simply jealous. Didn't like it that he got on television."

"Was it the people in the English department who felt that way?" Turner asked.

"I suspect most of them. The worst was the chairman Atherton Sorenson. I think if he could have stopped Giles from getting tenure, he would have."

"Did they fight?" Fenwick asked.

"No one at the University of Chicago 'fights,' " she said.

"They declare war. You may never see a shot fired, but they'll tear each other to pieces in a thousand ways."

"If his chairman hated him, how'd he get tenure?" Fenwick asked.

"Giles was alderman after the issue of tenure came up. Giles had the research and publications and connections at the University. I never heard that his getting tenure was a major problem." She smiled. "We secretaries know a lot but not everything."

"Who was his best friend on the faculty?" Turner asked.

She thought for a minute. "I'm not sure you'd say he had friends on the faculty. Many of them went to the Quadrangle Club every day for lunch, and many of them vied to sit with the chairman, but Gideon never seemed to have one buddy. Certainly I never heard of him going out with one of the members of the department for a drink. I don't know if they had a lot of dinner parties at his home."

"Did he have any enemies besides Atherton?" Fenwick asked.

"No more or less than anybody else."

"Grudges? Simmering feuds? Everyone else at the University described the department as a veritable Eden. You mentioned the head of the department, Sorenson, anybody at all? What about Darcy Worthington and Otto Kempe, the two professors in the English department?"

She thought carefully. "Two things stand out in my mind, but really I think they were nothing."

Turner urged her to tell anyway.

"Well, as for Worthington, I'm sure it's really nothing."

"What was it?" Fenwick urged.

"Well, when Giles started, he and Darcy were real close." She repeated much of the same story that Worthington had told Turner on Tuesday. At the end she added, "They kind of acted like it was all made up, but I'm not sure I ever saw them together once, all the time I worked there. I don't know, sometimes I thought some bad feelings remained." She could remember no concrete examples of this occurring.

"What about Kempe?" Turner asked.

"Really, it couldn't have been anything," she said.

"Tell us anyway," Fenwick said.

"Well, Kempe used to tease Giles about being friendly rivals. Now that I think about all the articles I typed for Giles, it seems like they always happened to be writing about the same subject at the same time. I don't know if that's odd or not. Another thing, Kempe could tell a thousand different jokes. At parties he could always be counted on to entertain everybody with absolutely marvelous stories. He was probably the most-liked person in the department."

"How did he get along with Giles?" Turner said.

"I always thought Gideon strained a bit to smile at the jokes and stories. Giles was the brunt of a few of the stories, but Kempe picked on everybody at some time or another. It wasn't really noticeable. I can't see it as being a big thing."

Turner asked her about Giles's and the health-food drinks.

"Is that what the poison was in?" she asked.

Turner nodded.

She gulped. "He always was bringing in these concoctions, each one more vile than the last. He constantly tried to get me to drink some. I know they were mostly vegetables and were good for me, but I could barely stand the smell of them. He usually drank something healthful after lunch."

"Who knew he did that?" Turner asked.

"I don't know. I never gave it much thought myself."

They spoke for a short while longer, but that was all she knew.

"Let's go talk to Darcy Worthington," Fenwick said.

Turner looked him up on his master list. Worthington lived in a high rise on South Shore Drive a block in from Lake Shore Drive. The security guard told them Worthington wasn't home.

They decided to try the Quadrangle Club to see if any of the people from the English department might be hanging around that popular establishment.

"What bugs me," Fenwick said, "is how the killer did it. That had to be an incredible chance, to walk in there and poison him."

"We've asked everybody about his eating habits. Everybody knew some version of the fact that he ate health foods. A few people thought he might have eaten things at regular intervals, but nobody knew for sure. Killer could have brought it in and walked off."

"Hell of a nerve," Fenwick said. "So it could have been anybody at any time during the day after he bought his ingredients. You'd think somebody would have seen a stranger."

"Don't forget, no one even saw Giles return from lunch, and nicotine can take a while to work, especially if Giles took it on a full stomach. He ate lunch some time in that hour before he died."

"Killer walks in, pours poison in his juice, and leaves. Could have been somebody from politics," Fenwick said, "but my bet is on somebody from the university. It would have been so much easier."

"Maybe the killer is counting on us to think that," Turner said.

At the Quadrangle Club they spotted Darcy Worthington taking advantage of the pleasantly cool spring day out on the tennis courts. Turner and Fenwick walked onto the playing surface. When Worthington noticed them at the edge of the court, he threw them a sneer and tried to ignore them. His opponent looked to be the age of a graduate student. Both wore warm-up suits. Worthington had a sweater tied around his waist. Fenwick stalked to the middle of the net and the game stopped. Worthington snarled, walked over to his gym bag, and grabbed a towel out of the top.

"What are you doing here?" Worthington asked.

"We need to ask you a few questions," Fenwick said.

The student walked over. Worthington thanked him for the game and told him he'd see him next week.

"You lied Tuesday," Turner said.

Worthington glared at him. He untied a sweater from around his waste and pulled it over his head. "I resent that remark," Worthington said.

"Tough shit," Fenwick said.

Worthington glanced around the tennis court. No one else was out in the early spring coolness.

"You can't talk to me that way," Worthington said.

Fenwick laughed. "Sure I can. I just did." He moved closer to Worthington and lowered his voice. "I can do just about anything I want."

"I won't put up with police brutality. You won't do anything here, in such a public place." You could see the tennis courts from numerous windows.

"Don't have to do it here," Fenwick said. "We could take a trip down to the station and bust up some of that arrogance."

"I knew the Chicago police were just thugs," Worthington said. He began to move away from them.

Fenwick placed his bulk in front of him. "This is a murder investigation, you stupid shit. We don't put up with lies from anybody. We want some truth, and we'll take it here or down at the station. You make the choice."

Worthington looked at Turner. "You can't do this," the professor said.

Turner said, "What really happened between you and Gideon Giles when you had your falling out?"

Worthington looked from one cop to the other. "You can't," he began. "I won't." Beads of sweat shone on his upper lip and forehead.

Fenwick put his nose an inch from Worthington's. The cop said, "You need to never tell me what I can or can't do. Right now I'm a cop who wants answers, and I better hear some real soon, and I better like what I hear."

Turner said, "Come on, Darcy. Just tell us what happened."

Worthington mopped at the sweat on his face. "Okay," he mumbled, "but not here."

They trekked to his office on the third floor of Swift Hall. The building was open and he didn't need to use his key to enter. The halls on this Saturday were deserted and quiet. In Worthington's office, Turner noted the hundreds of books crammed into shelves that filled three of the walls. Worthington tossed his gym bag in a corner and sat behind a paper-strewn desk.

"I didn't kill him," he said.

"What happened, Darcy?" Turner asked. "Why'd you guys fight?"

Worthington used the edge of a paperback book to clean under his nails. He fiddled with the collar of his warm-up suit. Finally he gazed at Turner for several minutes before telling his story.

Worthington and Giles had hit it off from the first day they joined the faculty. As the only two new people in the department that year, they found themselves thrown together, sharing experiences. "We'd go out together, drinking buddies. We'd meet with students, talk for hours, work out, go running along the lakefront. We'd get together with our wives and spend hours talking and laughing. We even took a few vacations with them. Those were the best days of my life." He pushed his chair back and put his feet on the desk. "In those days I wanted to make a difference in the world. I wanted to excite young minds. And kids here are bright. They don't need to be taught how to think. I thought I could change the world. I always figured Gideon Giles shared those dreams. All those talks we had, I don't know how I didn't notice." He paused.

"Notice what?" Turner said.

"That Gideon Giles was the most self-centered, ambitious creep I'd ever known. We got interested in local politics. Even worked in a few campaigns together, but you could almost see it, like a horrible disease, it took him over completely. He does have a certain presence in front of crowds. People listened to him. As his ambitions grew, the less he had to do with me. I enjoyed liberal politics, especially when it got the goat of some of the staid old-timers around here, but it became a religion to Giles, all-consuming. He had no time for those of us who'd known him."

He took his feet off the desk. Placed his elbows on his knees, and clasped his hands. He looked up at the cops. "So, I confronted him. Told him our friendship was more important to me than all this political power. He laughed at me." Worthington shook his head. "That laugh told me more than anything he could have said. It wasn't cruel, more total indifference. He didn't care if I existed or not."

He sighed deeply. "That wasn't the end of it. I couldn't let it go. He'd been my friend, the guy I'd been closest to in my whole life. I demanded he talk to me. I told him what I saw, tried to remind him of all the dreams we'd shared together. He turned vicious. No one witnessed this scene, so you see I'm being honest with you. We lost our tempers. We threatened each other. I made wild claims about how he'd be sorry. It was stupid, childish, but I was hurt."

"So you didn't just drift apart like you told us the other day," Fenwick said.

Worthington shook his head.

"When did all this happen?" Turner asked.

"Just after he was elected alderman the first time."

"What happened after the confrontation?" Turner asked.

"Nothing. It was in his office. I walked out. It was a Saturday, I remember, like this, with no one around, so no one heard us. Afterwards we were correct and polite with each other. We never did another thing together again."

164

He sat up in the chair. "And that was years ago. I had no reason to kill him. He was no threat to me. I had a secure job here."

"Did he ever have any other violent confrontations?" Turner asked.

"Not with anybody at the University. I've thought about this a lot since Tuesday. Trying to think who could have done it and what motive they would have had."

Your amateur sleuths in mysteries could get wound up in figuring out the motivation of the killer, but in actual fact, most of the time detectives ignored motive. What was far more important was physical evidence, witnesses, and confessions. A detective was far more likely to solve a case by figuring out how the killer did it than why. Sometimes there wasn't a why.

Worthington continued, "The only thing I could come up with was the night Giles won the election for committeeman. We weren't friends anymore, but some of us from the University wanted to go, see what it was like. On Giles's way up to the podium, this young woman stopped him. Remember now, the room was jammed, people shouting, laughing, band playing, but I saw the two of them clearly. She grabbed onto his arm and wouldn't let go. At first I thought it was simply someone trying to get a favor. I couldn't hear them, but it was obvious she wasn't saying congratulations. She waved her fist at him. He tried to pull away from her. Finally a couple of his campaign workers noticed and dragged the two of them apart. They escorted her to the door."

"Who was it?" Turner asked.

"I asked around. Somebody finally told me it the old committeeman's granddaughter, Molly McGee."

They talked for a few more minutes. Fenwick and Turner decided to take one more look at the crime scene in case they might have missed something, so they hung back as Worthington started down the corridor. At the top of the stairs he looked back. He was about twenty feet from them, his face in shadow.

"You know," he called back, "the person you should really talk to is Laura Giles. She really loved him. I can't believe the way he changed didn't affect her."

They listened to his receding steps. Giles's office still had the "police scene" tape across it. The door was locked. They spent fifteen minutes hunting for a security guard to open it for them. The woman who let them in seemed inclined to linger, but Fenwick asked her to leave. They'd find her when they were done so she could lock up. She left.

Turner sat on the desk in Giles's office. He watched Fenwick prowl around the room. His partner inspected the refrigerator, now emptied of its contents, all safely tucked away at the evidence lab. Fenwick gazed out the window at the quadrangle, inspected the desk, opened all the drawers, got down on his hands and knees and inspected the rug.

"Not much here," he said.

"Not much more the day of the murder," Turner said.

"Guard's coming back," Fenwick said.

Turner heard the soft footfalls. They both turned toward the door. A shadow appeared in the entryway to the outer office and stopped.

"What the fuck?" Fenwick said.

The barrel of a gun swung around the doorway. Turner dove for the floor. Shots rang out. Turner scrapped the knuckles on his right hand scrambling behind the desk. More shots thundered above him. Wood and plaster flew around the room.

Gun out, he raised the barrel above the edge of the desk top and returned fire.

Above the din he could occasionally hear Fenwick bellowing. "Fuck, double fuck, and triple fuck."

Turner emptied all twelve rounds toward the doorway. He yanked his gun back behind the desk to reload. Silence.

"Buck?" Turner called. He heard grunts and the sound of

clothing scraping against the floor. Buck's head appeared around the left side of the desk. "You okay?" Turner asked.

"Not as good as I'm going to be when I get that bastard." They listened carefully but didn't hear any sounds beyond their own breathing. Carefully, Turner raised an eyebrow and his gun over the edge of the desk. He heard Fenwick calling in their situation.

Eventually they decided it was safe enough to venture forth. They met their reinforcements at the head of the stairs. An hour and a half followed, filled with explanations, on-the-spot paperwork, and interviews with the all the brass that showed up.

The Area Ten commander arrived. Half an hour later, Turner and Fenwick walked out. The last thing the commander said to them was, "Find out what is behind all this. I don't care how many people you have to use. This is madness."

Turner and Fenwick sat in the car. "I was scared," Fenwick said.

"Me too," Turner said.

They'd been friends many years. It didn't bother them to admit the truth to each other. They sat in silence for fifteen minutes, enjoying the comfort of each other's presence. Finally Fenwick shook his head. "I'm hungry."

Turner looked at his watch. "Nearly seven."

"Missed Jeff's game," Fenwick said.

"Yeah," Turner said. "He's got one tomorrow night. I've missed too many family things lately."

"I know how it is," Fenwick said.

And Turner knew that Fenwick did know how it was, and he was content with his partner's sympathy, but the feeling of absence from his boys gnawed at him.

"I'm hungry," Fenwick repeated.

"You can eat at a time like this?" Turner asked.

"I've never had a time exactly like this," Fenwick answered. "When I got shot in the butt ten years ago, I was embarrassed and in pain. Now I'm hungry enough to eat the contents of a bakery early on a Sunday morning. The more creamed-filled doughnuts the better."

They settled on Ann Sathers on Fifty-seventh Street.

"We got Kempe, Molly McGee, and Laura Giles to see," Fenwick said over his third dessert.

"We'll have to roll you to the interviews," Turner said.

"You should eat more chocolate," Fenwick said. "It's disgusting when a guy in his mid thirties hasn't started putting on excess weight."

Turner wasn't up to debating metabolism. "It's Saturday night. I'm tired, still a little shook, but I want to follow this up now."

"We could get shot at again," Fenwick said.

Turner said, "So, we solve the case. Problems over."

Fenwick gazed at him carefully and said, "No guts, no glory."

They started at McGee's house. At eight-thirty Saturday night only a dim light shone from upstairs.

"Getting colder," Fenwick said, as he gave the door several more significant knocks. Turner watched his breath form steam.

Someone switched on a light in the foyer. Brightness gleamed through the strips of stained glass windows on either side of the entrance.

Molly McGee opened the door. "My grandfather's asleep," she told them.

"We need to talk to you," Turner said.

She looked confused but let them in. She led them to the room they'd talked to her grandfather in. She sat in the chair her grandfather had been in several nights before. She wore loose blue jeans and a turquoise sweater. She curled one foot under her. "What do you need?" she asked softly.

The room seemed to call for near whispers. Turner responded quietly, "We understand you had words with Gideon Giles?"

"Yes. Years ago. So what? It's not a secret. Half the people in the ward saw me."

"What was it about?" Turner asked.

She shut her eyes and threw back her head. When she opened her eyes, Turner thought they were icy with hate. "I said to him that night, that he was an unprincipled piece of dirt and that I hoped he died a horrible and lingering death. I didn't kill him," she said. "I didn't even see him that day when he came to talk to my grandfather."

Fenwick spoke in his normal tone. It sounded like trumpets in an outhouse. "Anybody could have gotten into his office from Monday morning until Tuesday at noon and poisoned his drink. Can you account for all your time for those twenty-four hours?"

"No," she said, "but I'd bet most of the people in this city would have a tough time coming up with a minute by minute remembrance of any day."

"Most of the people in the city didn't hate Gideon Giles the way you did," Fenwick said.

"I didn't kill him," she said, "and neither did my grandfather, who did a great deal for this city and deserves to be left alone."

The door to the library slowly swung open. A spectral figure hovered at the edge of the light.

"Molly, what is this?" Mike McGee tottered toward them. He wore a silk bathrobe over pajama bottoms. His slippered feet felt their way across the carpet. Molly jumped up and rushed toward him. She lead him to his chair. He gazed at the detectives.

"Mr. Turner and Mr. Fenwick," the old man said. "And why are you here?" McGee asked.

Turner explained.

"You think my Molly killed him, because of what that sniveling, lying, wise guy did to me? No, I would have done it myself. I hate him far more than Molly possibly could. If you're looking for hatred as a motive, then I'm your man, not Molly."

"Begging your pardon, sir," Turner said, "but we're looking for opportunity. With all due respect, you don't get around all that well. You couldn't have possibly snuck into the University and placed poison into Giles's drink. It needed someone quick and daring who could blend in with the other university students. Molly fits that."

"But she wasn't seen there, was she?" McGee asked.

"No," Turner admitted.

"Found any of her fingerprints?" McGee asked.

"Fingerprints were mostly a mess," Turner admitted. "We have Giles's and lots of random others. We could try matching hers."

Mike McGee tottered to his feet. He thrust a boney finger toward Turner. "How dare you! In my own home! Accuse my granddaughter! How dare you! Get out!"

His thin voice was high and raspy. Near the end he could barely gasp the words out. Molly rushed to him, comforted him, held him.

She glared at the detectives. Turner returned the gaze calmly.

They all listened to Mike McGee recover his composure. Finally, Molly McGee took her grandfather's hand and said, "I'd be happy to be fingerprinted. Mine won't match any there. I haven't been in Giles's office." She looked at the cops spitefully. "They are accusing me, and I know I can prove them wrong."

"Won't find her fingerprints," Fenwick said in the car.

"I wish she made a better suspect, but she's not really more likely than a lot of other people. We can't just start fingerprinting the entire Fifth Ward.

Turner called into the station. He talked to the watch commander. No news.

When he was done, he said to Fenwick, "It's nine-thirty. Late to go questioning," Turner said.

"I don't give a fuck if it's four in the morning. I want to talk to every single one of these shits."

They drove to Kenwood Avenue and down to the Giles's home. Alex Hill, Giles's brother-in-law, answered the door. He held it open but didn't invite them in. "It's late," he said.

"We're sorry," Turner said, "but we need to talk to Laura Giles."

Hill led them through an entryway still filled with winter coats on hooks. He opened another door to a living room. He asked them to sit. He would tell his sister they were here.

The room had a black leather couch with two matching love seats grouped around a glass-topped coffee table. One wall had a massive stereo system, silent now. The wall opposite the electronics had shelves filled with knickknacks and paperback books.

Laura Giles entered. She wore a severe black dress, and carried a box of pastel-colored tissues. She sat on the couch. Her brother started to sit next to her.

"We'd like to talk to you alone, Mrs. Giles," Turner said.

Hill glared at him, but Laura Giles put her hand on her brother's arm. She nodded at him. He left.

Turner and Fenwick sat on either side of her on the love seats.

Turner apologized for the lateness of the visit.

She waved this away calmly.

They asked if she'd remembered anything that might help them in their investigation, especially in terms of Giles's health-food beverages, but she told them she hadn't thought of anything new.

Fenwick asked, "We understand, Mrs. Giles, that your husband had changed over time, especially at the time he got involved in politics. Could you tell us about that?"

"Changed?" She looked thoughtful for a minutes. "I think some others saw him as this man who emerged from the quiet world of academia to the bright light of ambition and power." She gave them a brief smile. "I always knew he was ambitious and driven. He told me about his high school years. He was president of one thing or another, his class, clubs. I think he loved the struggles at the University. The power games everybody tried to pretend didn't happen. It just wasn't enough for him."

"Did he change toward you?" Turner asked.

"I don't think so. Over time we saw each other less, but we both had careers. I was always deeply involved in his campaigns. Someone told you that we didn't get along?"

"When one person moves to a big new position, sometimes it's hard for the rest of the family to adjust," Fenwick said.

"We had no children," Mrs. Giles said. "I had my career."

They left a few minutes later.

"Big nothing," Fenwick said in the car. "Where's Kempe live?"

Kempe lived in the Beverly neighborhood, a block west of the corner of 111th Street and Longwood Drive. The exterior was English Tudor. Kempe greeted them in stocking feet, gray slacks, and a smoking jacket. Turner apologized for the lateness of the visit. Kempe pulled a pipe out of his mouth and invited them in.

A long hallway with an antique Oriental rug and a granite ledge, led to a living room with carved wood sculptures of medieval monks above the fireplace, an antique Persian rug, ivory-colored sofas in silk and cotton, and soft peach walls. On the opposite wall from the fireplace, a stereo system softly played classical music.

Kempe stopped at a pipe holder in the middle of the fireplace mantle, took out a pouch, refilled his pipe, and sat down.

"What can I do for you gentlemen?" he asked.

He busied himself with tamping down his tobacco and lighting his pipe.

"It was more than friendly rivalry with Giles, wasn't it?" Fenwick asked.

Kempe stopped waving out a match and glared at him. A second later, he said, "Ouch," and flung the still-glowing remnant into the fireplace.

"I don't know what you mean," Kempe said.

"Cut the crap," Fenwick said. "Tell us what really happened."

"I told the truth on Tuesday. My God, I tried to save that man's life. I pounded on his chest, put my lips to his to try and breath life into him."

Turner said, "We've been told your rivalry was a great deal more than what you lead us to believe. We need to clear that up."

"Who's been talking?"

The cops didn't answer.

"What goes on in the University should stay in the University. We have no need for outside interference."

Turner said, "We'd like you to tell us what really happened between the two of you."

"I suppose you've talked to half the backbiters in the department, haven't you," Kempe said. "Jealousy is rife among those fools. We used to have a pretty laid-back department. Everybody like a family, willing to go out of their way for the other. It's changed like everything else. I think it all started when they moved part of the department up to the third floor of Swift Hall years ago. They should never have separated us."

"What happened between you and Gideon Giles, Mr. Kempe?" Turner asked.

"All right. It was probably that Atherton Sorenson who told.

173

I wouldn't put it past him. He's going to retire in a few years. Some of us manage to think ahead. We want to plan for an orderly succession. He doesn't like me. Thinks I'm scheming for his job." He puffed on his pipe until it went out.

The detectives waited in silence.

"All right. Giles was a thief. Every time I turned around he'd be topping me. If I had article coming out in *Chaucer Monthly,* he always seemed to have one the month before in *The Chaucer Review.* I never openly accused him of cheating, stealing my research or ideas. It'd sound like a petty departmental jealousy. For a while it was quite a joke. He never duplicated my research, but if I'd come to a unique conclusion based on true scholarship, he seemed to have the same thing based on little more than pure whimsy."

"If journals published his materials, he must have had research to support his conclusions," Turner said.

Kempe pointed the stem of his pipe at Turner. "You make an interesting point. Yes, his research was there, but where did he get it? Did he steal it from some graduate student? That's been known to happen. I joked with him to his face, but I knew him for the snake he was. I watched him like a hawk. After you people went through his papers, someone in the department called Mrs. Giles to see if she wanted them. She didn't. So I volunteered to go through them. I found what I was looking for. Proof that the rat had been cheating for years."

"You didn't find this out for sure until after the murder?" Fenwick asked.

"Right, but I knew him well for the conniver he was. For a while I thought he was trying to undermine me in departmental meetings. Always seemed to take the opposite side from me. I was too smart for him. I began waiting until he had made his position clear, then I'd make my move."

"Isn't this all just a little overdramatic?" Fenwick asked.

"This is only a university. I thought you guys were supposed to be reading books, studying, educating, all that."

Kempe chose not to condescend to Fenwick. He put his pipe aside, rubbed his right index finger under his nose. "I've been thinking about this since the murder. I'm afraid you're more than right. Being a university professor should be one of the most delightful jobs on earth. Some of us make it into a vicious gossiping society. We've got to change."

They asked him about Laura Giles, but he'd only met her at faculty functions, and they had spoken little more than beyond what was polite.

They talked for a while longer. They couldn't get Kempe to go beyond his admission that the rivalry between him and Giles had been intense.

It was after eleven. At Area Ten headquarters, they turned in the unmarked car. Turner found stacks of paperwork and two messages on his desk. The top note was from Ian. He had set up a meeting with the heads of numerous liberal groups for noon the next day.

The bottom one was from Clark Burke. He tossed it among the mounds of paper on his desk. He could fuss with the love-struck nineteen-year-old tomorrow.

E I G H T

Paul trudged up the steps into his house. No lights shone here
or in Mrs. Talucci's next door. He'd worked nearly sixteen
hours every day since Tuesday. His shoulders sagged, his head
drooped. He used his key to unlock the front door. He felt for
the light switch to the right and flicked it on. The brass lamp
on the end table nearest the door shone dimly.

Turner halted. Giovanni Parelli sat in the brown overstuffed
chair. Recliner pulled out, feet resting on it, Parelli gave him
a smile. Turner saw even white dentures. He gazed at the dark
brown eyes, the only real color in the gray ashen face.

"Who let you in?" Paul asked. He glanced toward Jeff's
room then toward the stairs and Brian's.

"Your boys are fine," Parelli said.

Paul glanced around the room. A noise from the kitchen

drew his attention. The burly guard shuffled into the room. Paul heard him dragging something behind him, then realized it was someone. The guard dumped Frank Ricken onto the couch.

"Dad." Brian appeared from in back of the guard. He had a red mark under his chin. "I tried to keep them out," Brian said. The guard didn't try to stop Brian from joining his dad near the door.

Paul examined his son's face. "Is Jeff all right?"

"Yeah. He's still asleep. They didn't bother him."

Paul turned to Parelli. "What is this?" he demanded. "How dare you break into my house?"

Parelli said, "I'm old. I'm sorry. I forget. I have news and I'm angry. Your son was overly vigorous in trying to keep us out. I'm sorry we hurt him. He's a good boy. Takes after his father. Wanted to protect his younger brother most of all. I wouldn't have come if it wasn't important. Again I apologize. Please sit down."

Paul tossed his coat on the back of the couch and sat on the armrest closest to Parelli. Brian stood behind him. The guard moved into the shadows of the hallway he'd just emerged from. Paul noted the rise and fall of Ricken's chest. In the soft light from the one lamp he could see a multitude of bruises on the right side of his face. Dark crimson patches stretched from shoulder to waist on the front of the shirt.

"Is he okay?" Paul asked.

"I'm told he will regain consciousness and will have a tremendous headache. The bruises you see. His wound was tended. He will be all right."

"What happened to him?" Turner asked.

"He was going to blow the whistle on our entire scheme," Parelli said. "I didn't know that. For Mrs. Talucci's sake, I will swear to you that I did not know that when you came to see me last night. I have no idea if you could possibly believe me. Maybe that isn't important."

The withered hands lifted several inches off his lap, palm outward.

"At any rate I was not told. People whose names I need not mention heard about it. They thought Mr. Ricken had to be stopped. They found this out Tuesday morning. He had gone to Mr. Giles late Monday night. Giles couldn't get hold of anyone that night. He called early Tuesday. We tried to find Mr. Ricken. He proved quite elusive. Then Giles was murdered. The news delayed the search for Ricken. Originally some people thought he'd done it. After the delay the search resumed. He put up more of a fight than anyone thought. He had to be frightened into silence. He didn't seem ready to listen to reason. People who were sent got rough. There is no need for violence in these matters. People simply need to be convinced."

"Why attack that media consultant Stimpson?" Paul asked.

"Ricken had told him. They planned to work together to expose Giles. Our people talked to Mr. Stimpson. He balked at first, but then saw the light of reason." The old head shook. Parelli ran a hand through his wisps of white hair. "I am too old for this sort of thing. I no longer have the stomach for such nonsense. I heard Mr. Stimpson has plans to leave town. Has a campaign in California to run."

"He was scared off," Paul said.

"Yes," Parelli said.

"What's to keep either of them from talking?" Paul asked.

"If the fools who attacked them had thought a minute, they would have known that with Giles dead, Ricken had no proof. He had no documentation. The one man who could prove his allegations was dead. There was no need for anyone to get beaten up. Ricken should have been talked to and shown the error of his ways, but younger more volatile people are in charge now. They don't understand how to use reason. Stimpson has no commitment to Chicago. He's an outsider who comes in to do jobs. He doesn't care about politics in this city."

178

"Why bring Ricken here?" Paul asked.

"As a peace offering, a way to show that what I'm telling you is the truth, and we have no use for the man. He can face whatever his problems are with neither threat nor help from us."

"Dad," Jeff's voice called from down the hall.

Paul pushed past the guard and hurried into Jeff's room. He'd have killed Parelli's guard if he'd tried to keep him from his son.

Jeff was trying to swing his legs off his bed and get into his wheelchair. Paul picked him up and carried him into the living room. Jeff sat blinking at the light.

"What's going on, Dad?" Jeff asked.

"I would never hurt your children," Parelli said. The old man gazed at the boy's withered legs.

"This man is a friend of Mrs. Talucci's," Paul said.

"Oh," Jeff said. He settled into his father's lap. "Why is he here so late?"

"He doesn't have as many manners as Mrs. Talucci," Paul said.

Jeff pointed to Ricken on the couch. "What's wrong with him?" the boy asked.

"He's an unlucky suspect in one of my investigations," Paul said.

"Is he a killer?" Jeff asked.

"No, son," Paul said. "He's a man who needs help."

Jeff yawned and snuggled his head onto Paul's shoulder. In a minute he fell asleep.

Parelli's soft voice said, "I am very sorry. I am old and foolish. I should not have come here."

"Somebody shot at me and my partner at the University of Chicago this afternoon," Paul said.

Parelli glanced at his guard. "I can place a few guards around you," Parelli offered.

Paul laughed. "I don't think the bad guys should be protecting the cops. Tell me why I'm being attacked."

"Same reason Ricken was attacked. The people who planned this are running scared. I didn't get to them until late this afternoon, obviously after they attacked you. I told them I had told you everything, and that I will talk to the press if you are not left alone. I see you now with your sons, and I wish I had memories of my father like that, but more, I promised Rose to keep you safe. A promise to Rose Talucci is more important to me than politics, especially at my age. You will not be harmed. You will not be bothered again. It has been taken care of."

"I don't want to owe you a favor," Paul said.

The old man looked pained. "Accept it that I am paying back more of my debt to Rose."

Paul nodded.

Parelli said. "You have your answer. The political situation did not require or need death as a solution. As far as we are concerned, Gideon Giles could still be alive. His death was a blow to our control of the city. He was not going to blow the whistle. Your murderer lies elsewhere."

"How can I be sure your people were telling you the truth?" Paul asked. "They lied to you before."

Parelli inclined his head toward his guard. "I had Barney convince them it was in their best interest to tell me the truth. They didn't kill Gideon Giles."

He rose to his feet. His bodyguard hurried to his side, but Parelli did not take the proffered assistance. Parelli said, "I again deeply apologize for inconveniencing you." He walked over to Paul and patted him on the shoulder. At the door Parelli said, "I leave you Mr. Ricken. I hope he has a more successful life in the future than he's had up to now. If he talks to the police or the press, I will make no move to stop him. People will have to pay for this blundering."

Paul carried Jeff back to bed. The boy murmured briefly when he left his father's arms, but didn't fully waken.

Paul called an ambulance. They arrived in fifteen minutes

and took Ricken away. Before the paramedics left, they confirmed to Paul that Ricken was in stable condition, but they would know more when he regained consciousness. Paul called the Twelfth District and told them to have a guard placed on Ricken at Cook County Hospital until he had a chance to talk to him in the morning.

After they left, Paul and Brian sat at the kitchen table. "I'm sorry they got in," Brian said. "I should have been able to protect the house better."

"You did fine, son. The guy's a professional. I want to wrap this case up, get back to you guys as much as possible. I haven't seen enough of you. I'm sorry."

"It's okay, Dad. I understand. Really."

Upstairs, ready to enter their separate bedrooms, Brian asked, "Did you really get shot at again?"

"Yeah," Paul said. "Let's talk about it in the morning." Minutes later Paul crawled into bed.

Loud banging intruded on his sleep. He opened an eye and saw daylight streaming through the bedroom window. His door opened and Brian stuck his head around the door.

"What?" Paul asked.

His older son strode across the room. He held the Sunday edition of the *Chicago Tribune*. Brian pointed at the front page. Paul read the headline COPS ATTACKED AT U OF C.

"Last night you only said you'd been shot at. You didn't say anything about an attack like this. Ben's downstairs. Mrs. Talucci's more furious than I've ever seen her. Ian's left two messages on the machine. You didn't hear the phone." Brian sat on the edge of the bed. "Why didn't you tell me last night?"

Paul rubbed his morning beard. "I didn't see the point last night in describing each shot."

"The paper talks about machine-gun fire," Brian said.

Paul sat up and took the paper from his son. "Didn't they see this on the news last night?"

"I only watched the sports scores. I guess none of them saw it either." Brian's eyes searched his father's anxiously. "Is everything really going to be all right?"

"There was no machine-gun fire," Paul said. "The reporter exaggerated a little here and there and conveniently left out a few things. Makes for a more exciting story." He put the paper down. "I would never let anything hurt you boys." Paul touched Brian's arm. "Nothing is more important to me in the world than you and Jeff. I couldn't be prouder of how you handled yourself last night or the way you're concerned about me now. Thanks."

He noted the beginning of a smile on his son's face. Brian said, "You better talk to the people in the kitchen pretty quick."

"If you could leave me in peace for a couple minutes, I'll get myself downstairs and greet the concerned masses."

Fifteen minutes later, showered and shaved, Paul walked into his kitchen. Ian was now present along with Brian, Jeff, Ben, and Mrs. Talucci. Questions flew for about two minutes, then Paul called for order.

Mrs. Talucci spoke firmly, "I have already spoken to Giovanni Parelli. He said he apologized last night. He will make restitution."

"I don't want anything from him," Paul said.

Paul asked if anyone wanted breakfast. Mrs. Talucci said she'd fix it. Paul tried to insist he'd make it. While he waited for breakfast, he called Fenwick. They agreed to meet at Area Ten at one. He outlined his meeting with Parelli.

"Okay," Fenwick said, "Giovanni thinks it wasn't the politicians. How do we know he isn't simply trying to take the heat off them?"

"We don't," Turner said. He told Fenwick he'd fill him in on all the details when they met.

Ian made a number of calls to the people in the reform

organizations. They agreed to pass the word that the meeting would take place at two-thirty instead of noon.

Over breakfast they all wanted to know every detail about the shooting.

"Were you scared, Dad?" Jeff asked at one point.

They all looked at Paul. "Very much so," he told his son.

"I'm glad you're okay," his younger son said.

"Me too," Ben said.

He managed to calm all their fears. He wondered when he'd have time to deal with his own. Ben caught him alone for a minute as Paul took his gun out of the safe in his bedroom.

"Are you okay?" Ben asked.

"Mostly." They hugged briefly. "We can talk about it later," he said. He promised to call Ben that night.

The trip to Cook County Hospital, just a few blocks away, took only a few moments. When Turner walked in, he found Ricken staring out the window of his room. He turned his head toward the door. Purple bruises shown out of his pale face. He looked only slightly better than last night.

"What happened?" Ricken asked.

Turner pulled up a hospital chair and told him about the events of the night before. Then he asked Ricken about the campaign manager's misadventures.

Ricken told a tale of abduction straight out of Beruit terrorism. "I was scared then, but I'm not going to let them get away with this."

Turner admired his courage, if not his intelligence.

"I'm going to fight this," Ricken said. "I lied to them yesterday. This isn't a totalitarian state. I'm going to expose them."

Turner had brought Ian with him. He called his friend in from the corridor. He left the two of them alone. Turner had made no promises to Parelli, felt no need to protect the man after his invasion of the house. And Parelli had said he wouldn't

183

intercede if Ricken went public. Turner doubted if any investigation would ever reach Parelli. The old man wasn't in charge anymore. Younger men had made some stupid decisions.

Turner was ten minutes late getting to Area Ten to meet Fenwick. They endured questions from half the people in the building about how the investigation was going. They responded respectfully and carefully to the questions from the watch captain and the area commander. These two made it clear that the pressure was still on, and they needed a suspect.

Turner and Fenwick talked to Wilson. She said, "I've interrogated all the people connected to the Gideon Giles campaign organization and ward office who got fired in the past year. I had Blessing upstairs run checks on all of them. Nobody struck me as a murder suspect. Since we don't know when they put the poison in, I couldn't very well pin them down to alibis for every minute after Monday morning. I still asked, but nobody stood out as a blatant liar. I think those people are a dead end."

They thanked her and trooped upstairs to ask Blessing if he had anything for them. Blessing, tie loosened, and looking like he hadn't slept, said, "I've got the campaign financial disclosure data here. I've cross-referenced it with all of our other data. I got one or two odd things." He led them over to his charts and began to explain.

Five minutes after he started, Fenwick said, "I'm lost already. Distill it. We've got a meeting in a few minutes."

"Two of the liberal organizations show up everywhere. The Anti-Fur people and the Save the Porpoises."

"Anti-Fur?" Fenwick asked.

"You know," Turner said. "They accost people on the street who wear animal skins."

"No porpoises in the Fifth Ward," Fenwick said.

Blessing ignored him. "What's odd is, we can't connect them to any legitimate group. We've got documentation on everybody else, but not on them. Other groups either gave money or got help, just like these, but they're all registered nice and proper like they're supposed to be, or at least have addresses that check out as legitimate. Took us nearly a day to track some of them down. These two don't check out."

"They're fake," Fenwick said.

"Vacant lots at the addresses. Money went back and forth. A few thousand each year. Could be dummy groups for shifting campaign money around illegally."

"I thought the anti-fur crowd was real," Turner said.

"They are," Blessing said, "it's just this branch of their group doesn't check out. I wouldn't call them fake. They're on paper, but they don't check out. It's something odd. Thought you might want to see it."

They thanked him for his detailed work. Before driving to their meeting, Turner returned Clark Burke's call from the night before. He asked Burke to meet him at the Sheridan Park Community Center at five. This was in the park a half block from the Turner home. Turner didn't tell Burke that was where Jeff had a game. The university student agreed to take the bus over and join him.

Ian had set up the meeting with the leaders of most of Giles's social welfare groups at the Buckingham Avenue Worker's Church. Large numbers of the organizations used the space there for meetings and other activities. Many of the city's famous liberals had come from the congregation.

Ian wasn't there. Turner assumed he was still with Ricken. He hoped his friend would show up before the end. Turner tried to find out which groups were which. He wanted to talk to the fur and porpoises set if they'd even bothered to show.

They met in the church auditorium. Two foot strips of alternating primary colors filled one wall. The stage was bare. Opposite the painted wall was a graffiti mural. It stretched from the front of the room to the back. Names, slogans, childlike drawings, plus community art from floor to ceiling.

Eventually Turner addressed the group. He explained the

police needed their help in gathering information about who might want to murder Giles, and by doing so, harm their causes. The two detectives listened to attacks on the police for not doing enough to solve the murder and not reaching out to various communities. Three people berated them for police brutality. Many of the people in the audience agreed that the murder was probably a conspiracy by right-wing, religious fundamentalists trying to hurt their causes.

Around four, Ian showed up. He joined Turner in front of the room. Ian whispered in his ear while a man with a white beard spoke about requiring classical music in all preschools and day-care centers.

Ian said, "Just got done with a press conference with Ricken. All the media were there. We're talking big time. I got a promise of some protection for the two of us for a while."

"Good thing," Turner said. "Parelli and his cronies might not want to hurt you, but I think there are other people who are still dangerous."

Ian glanced out at the crowd. "Why hasn't Fenwick arrested all of them yet? I was kind of hoping he would."

Turner looked at Fenwick. For all his partner's volatility, he knew he'd be calm. They stressed in cops' training about diffusing tense situations, instead of turning them into conflagrations. He'd seen Fenwick in the middle of tough spots when crowds had begun to gather after an arrest. Fenwick had earned commendations for his behavior at those points.

Turner whispered back to Ian, "He puts it on cruise control. He gets angry with witnesses and suspects, but he's never ruined an arrest because of it."

Turner told Ian he wanted to talk to anybody connected with the Anti-Fur and Save the Porpoises groups. Ian scanned the crowd. "Call a recess," he said. "I know who most of these people are, but I can find somebody who knows everybody."

Five minutes later the man with the beard sat down. Turner quickly rose and called for a pause. As the room broke up into scattered groups, Ian led the two cops to a woman in white jeans and a gray shirt with a clerical collar. Ian introduced her as the pastor of the church and explained what the detectives wanted to know.

She said, "I worked closely with most of these people and the Giles campaign. I know everyone in the room. I've never seen or heard of an organization called Anti-Fur or Save the Porpoises." She introduced the detectives to the leaders of the Anti-Cruelty and the Save the Whales groups, but none of them had heard of the groups Turner and Fenwick wanted.

The meeting ended a few minutes later. Outside the church, Turner thanked Ian for setting up the conference on such short notice. "What's going to happen with Ricken?" Turner asked.

"I'm going to win another Pulitzer Prize," Ian said. "We are going to need a lot more proof." He sighed. "Ricken has this odd view that if you put it on television, all the true and right people will win. He's read too many of his own press releases. We'll get lots of pressure on the politicians because of the press conference, but what we really need is a few more people who did the actual infiltrating to come forward. I've got a hot lead on that." Ian left.

"The meeting was a disaster," Fenwick said as they drove to Area Ten. "I didn't know I was a 'boar hunting beast of the primeval forest.'"

"I've been meaning to talk to you about that," Turner said.

"Very funny."

"Who called you that?"

"Who remembers? And who cares?" They drove in silence the rest of the way to Area Ten. Fenwick turned off the engine. Neither of them moved to get out of the car.

"Now what?" Fenwick asked.

Turner said, "I go home, pick up Jeff, and we go to his basketball game. I have no ideas on the case. We can send Blessing and his computers hunting for these fake liberal groups. He's probably already tried everything possible to check them out. We've talked to most of the suspects and witnesses at least twice. We've tried every lead and every possibility. The commander, the press, and the politicians can scream their heads off, but we ain't got nothin'. And I for one am going to have some time for my family."

Minutes later, Turner walked into his house. Brian was on the phone. From what the seventeen year old said, it sounded like he was trying to convince a date to join him at the basketball game.

Jeff was in his room. He'd changed into his warm-up suit with ROLLING ROCKETS emblazoned in bright red on the front.

"You coming to the game, Dad?" Jeff asked.

"Sure am."

"Ben said he was going to try and make it. I hope I get to play more this time."

Brian, at the door to the room, said, "Just try your best, squirt."

"Are you bringing Marcia?" Jeff asked his older brother.

"Said she'd be there."

"I like her," Jeff said.

"Have I met Marcia?" Paul asked. "Do I want to meet Marcia?"

"She's just another one of Brian's girlfriends," Jeff said, "but she brought me popcorn and a Coke at the last game. She was nice."

They arrived fifteen minutes before the game was to start. Ben met them in the parking lot of the field house. Paul walked in with Jeff on his shoulders. His younger son waved and called to his friends rushing about the court shooting baskets, warming up for the game.

Clark Burke sat on the bottom row of the bleachers. He saw Paul and stood up, giving him a mystified look. Paul introduced him to Jeff, Ben, and Brian.

Burke looked at all three of them quizzically. "You have two sons?" Burke asked.

"Yeah," Brian said, "it makes him feel macho."

A pretty blonde-haired girl waved to Brian from across the court. Brian practically loped over to her. Paul talked to the coach and the parents, most of whom he knew. He met Marcia. She smiled shyly at him and greeted him politely. Paul liked her already.

Even Myra, ace mechanic, showed up to cheer Jeff on.

The game began. Paul sat between Ben and Burke. The college student looked confused. During a break in the action he asked softly, "Why am I here?"

"I wanted you to meet my sons and my lover," Paul said.

"Oh," Burke said. He was very quiet for most of the rest of the game, although he did tell Turner early on that the campus police had two suspects in the trashing of Burke's room. They were a couple of neo-Nazis who'd seen his name connected with the Gideon Giles investigation. They'd planned on attacking some gay person on campus, but figured he'd be more vulnerable and shook up if they attacked now.

"How they catch them?" Turner asked.

Burke told him that the guys had tried to trash another dorm room, but many of the floors had banded together to provide a crime watch on each floor. "They practically walked into a trap," Burke said.

Turner told Burke he was glad they caught the guys and hoped that would be the end of the problem. "What about your computer?" Turner asked.

"Everything they wrecked, they're going to have to pay for."

Jeff got to play for five minutes and scored his first basket in a game. His team won by eight points. After the game Jeff twirled his wheelchair around and around the basketball court.

"Did you see that, Dad?" he called when he calmed down enough to talk to people.

Paul hugged his son and congratulated him. Jeff and Brian exchanged a complicated series of handshakes. Myra hugged Jeff and kissed him on the forehead, but said she had other plans so couldn't stop for the victory party.

Paul insisted Burke accompany them to the house for a postgame celebration. Burke wound up walking ahead with Brian and Jeff.

Paul unzipped his jacket and took a deep gulp of the fresh spring breeze. "This is beautiful," he said.

Ben murmured to Paul, "Are you sure you want to bring him along?"

"Yes, he's got a puppy crush on me. I figure it'll save him some embarrassment. He hasn't asked me for a date or declared his love. This way he sees how I live, you, the boys. I think he's a decent kid. He hasn't had a lot of chances to socialize with an older group of gay people. He's had his peers, which can sometimes be more unsettling to the ego than anything else."

They sat in the kitchen, laughed and talked, ate hot dogs and beans. Clark seemed to become more at ease after Jeff asked if he was a murder suspect and Paul told him no, that he was someone he'd met at the beginning of the investigation at the University.

Ben left a few minutes after seven. Paul left Brian and Jeff to clean the kitchen. He sat with Burke in the living room.

"This is really nice," Burke said.

Paul thanked him. Silence fell between them. Paul let it build.

Burke sat on the couch, clasping and unclasping his hands. He said, "Thank you for not letting me make a fool out of myself."

"You're welcome," Paul said.

"Brian and Jeff know you're gay?" Burke asked.

"You'll be able to tell your family someday," Paul said.

"I hope so."

Paul asked how his new room was. Burke seemed pleased with it. Burke brought up the murder and asked how the investigation was going. Paul outlined some of what they'd done.

"It's still scary when I think about it."

Later Brian offered to drive Burke home. Clark turned him down, but accepted a ride when Paul made a similar suggestion a few minutes later. Paul drove the college student to the dorm. They talked little. As Burke got out of the car, he said, "Thanks for inviting me. I'm glad I met all those people."

Turner decided to stop in Area Ten before returning home. It was only a few blocks out of the way. He wanted to see if there'd been any developments connected with Ricken. At the admitting desk they told him nothing had been reported on the murder, but that the campaign finance irregularities had already been assigned to a special unit at 11th and State.

The squad room was deserted. On the fourth floor he found Blessing tapping the keys of a computer. The cop gave him a nod of hello and said nothing new had come in. Turner wandered over to the wall displays. He'd gone over Blessing's chart of people. Now he gazed at the hundreds of campaign brochures displayed on one of the other walls. He studied them idly.

Blessing eased up next to him. "It's something, isn't it," he said.

Turner nodded.

"I put them up in order by years. The ones you're looking at are from the first campaign."

Turner saw a younger Gideon Giles and his wife shaking hands, posing in front of significant landmarks in the neighborhood. The two cops wandered down the wall examining them.

"Funny," Turner said when he'd gone through several years. "After the first year or so, Mrs. Giles stops turning up."

Blessing joined him. For an hour they minutely inspected all of the propaganda documents.

"She's not in any of them for the past six years," Turner said.

"Why is that odd?" Blessing asked.

"Mrs. Giles told us she was very involved in her husband's campaigns. You got all that stuff up here we took from Giles office at the University?"

Blessing directed him to a stack of cartons, each labeled by its contents. It took several minutes for Turner to find the box with the materials from the top of Giles's desk. "No photo of him and his wife," Turner said, "and I'm sure there wasn't one."

"Everybody has a picture of themselves and their wives and kids on their desk?" Blessing said.

"People like to personalize the space they occupy," Turner said. "I've got pictures of my kids on my desk. Fenwick has one of his family. Do you?"

Blessing nodded.

"It's a normal thing, but this guy had nothing. I think I want to talk to Laura Giles again."

He called Fenwick and told him what he had found.

Fenwick showed up a half hour later. Together they drove to the Giles's home. Alex Hill opened the door. He glowered at them, but led them to the living room.

Lilac Ostergard sat on the black leather couch next to Laura Giles, holding her hand. Laura Giles looked at the two detectives and shuddered.

"Want me to throw them out?" Alex asked.

"Alex, if you could wait in the den," she said. "I'll talk to you later." She said this quietly and without anger. Alex hesitated, but Lilac gave him a sharp look and he left.

Lilac said, "Do you want me to go, Laura?"

"No, stay, please," she said. She looked at the two cops.

"Why aren't you in any of your husband's campaign literature for the past six years?" Turner asked.

"You don't have to talk to these men," Lilac said.

Laura Giles whispered, "I felt so shut out."

"You lied to us when you said you worked closely with him in his campaigns?" Turner asked.

Turner could barely hear her murmur, "Yes."

"You went to his office on Monday, didn't you?" Turner asked.

Laura Giles body quivered. She grabbed a tissue from the box on the coffee table. Tears streamed down her cheeks.

"I knew his secretary was gone on vacation. If I saw anyone, I could just say I was there to see Gideon, but nobody was around. I found his supply of health-food drinks. I poured in the poison and ran. I was petrified that someone would see me on the way out. No one did. A few minutes later I met him in the quadrangle for lunch."

Laura Giles told how she had endured her husband's increasing coldness and cruelty for years. "It had been building for years. I was loyal and helpful during all that time. I had that fatuous politician's wife look down perfectly. He used me all up. I'd done everything right, and he dumped me. It would have been better if there was another woman. It made me even angrier because I was competing against his ambition. I could fight another woman, but I didn't know how to fight his career.

"He just didn't care for me and, like a stupid fool, I still loved him. I was addicted to him, and the more he deprived me of his love, the more I needed it." She continued in a whisper. "All the years we worked together, and he told me last week he wanted a divorce. He hadn't told any one yet, because he wanted to think about how it would affect his political chances. Not because he loved me, but because of how it would hurt his goddamned career."

Later at Area Ten, Turner avoided the brass that showed up, and dodged the press.

They did enough paperwork to satisfy the needs of the arrest and left the rest of it until the morning.

Turner found both of his boys in the front room watching television. "Little late for a school night, Jeff," Paul said.

"We saw on television where you solved the murder," Jeff said.

"Ian was on too," Brian said. "With the guy who was here last night. They said they had the biggest scandal to hit the city in years. Was that part of the murder?"

Paul gave brief explanations. He tucked Jeff into bed, gave his son an extra hug. In the living room he found Brian reading a book. His son looked up. "Jeff finally calm down?" he asked.

"He scored his first basket. He'll be in heaven for days."

"Or until his next game," Brian said.

Paul got up. "Don't stay up too late," he said.

Brian nodded. As Paul reached the bottom step to go up to his room and catch up on his sleep, Brian called, "Dad."

Paul looked back at his son.

"I'm glad you're okay," Brian said.

Paul smiled. "Me too. See you in the morning."